A REASON TO KILL

AMANITA — a genus of mushroom which is a study in contrast. It contains the most deadly and the most delicious species of fleshy fungi.

A REASON TO KILL

by

Eve Zaremba

An Amanita Publication

CANADIAN CATALOGUING IN PUBLICATION DATA

Zaremba, Eve
A reason to kill

2nd ed.
First published: Markham, Ont.: Paperjacks, 1978.
"A Helen Keremos mystery."
ISBN 0-921299-08-7
I. Title.
PS8599.A74R42 1989   C813'.54   C89-093901-2
PR9199.2.Z37R42 1989

Cover and Book Design by Elizabeth Martin
Typesetting by Third Generation Graphics Ltd.
Printing by Webcom
Amanita Logo Design by Dougal Haggart

SECOND EDITION 1989
PRINTED AND BOUND IN CANADA

ORDER INFORMATION:

Amanita Enterprises
P.O. Box 784, Station P
Toronto, Ontario, Canada
M5S 2Z1

Preface

A Reason to Kill was first published in 1978. Working backwards, I finished it in 1977, started it in 1976 and first had the idea in 1975. That's almost fifteen years ago; in current parlance, 'that's history, man': dismissable. These days it seems that almost nobody cares about history, not even about our own past. Gay people are no different in this respect from everyone else. Rather than recall the way it really was—or the way it seemed to us—then, we wallow in manufactured nostalgia. The twenties, the forties, the sixties, even the very recent seventies have all become that romantic Time Before AIDS.

Well, *A Reason to Kill* ain't romantic. There is no mistaking that it was written back in the seventies and not just set in that era. It is about homophobia, coming-out, gay self-hatred, betrayal, murder, all manifested exclusively through the lives of a couple of young gay men—yet written by a lesbian! Who would dare do that now! Helen Keremos, the detective, is a middle-aged dyke, an anomaly in the seventies when any of us over 27 were definitely 'older'. She was one of the the very first of her kind. There are now lesbian mysteries published by our own presses, but not many with dykes as professional detectives. And, fifteen years later, not one mainstream publisher has produced a mystery series with a lesbian private eye.

I did not know at the time that I was writing a 'seventies' book or breaking any new ground. One doesn't. I set out to write a mystery well within the tradition of the genre, with a hard-nosed, apolitical detective/outsider, who happened to be lesbian. I have never been interested in producing a romantic adventure or a coming-out story disguised as a mystery. That's for someone else to write. And I don't intend Helen to be politically correct. PIs are p.i. by definition.

When I started *A Reason to Kill* I didn't know whether I could produce a lesbian private eye character who felt true to me, give her a good mystery to solve and make the whole thing work. For a mystery maven like me the plot, the story, the case are the thing. So it happens that mystery buffs have liked my books well enough. But some who are new to the genre and not familiar with its conventions, or those who expect more overt feminist content or more sex, have been downright outraged. Needless to say, I've had to dodge a lot of flak. However since there are now three Helen Keremos mysteries (and another taking shape in my word processor) the Yeah!s beat out the Nah!s.

The (new) book in my wp will include more of Helen's personal life, including sex, a 'relationship' and other trivia. For whether it's the seventies, eighties or nineties as far as I am concerned it's the mystery that matters. I hope you will enjoy this one. Not a word has been changed from the first edition in 1978.

Eve Zaremba
Toronto, April 1989

1

THE PARKING LOT WAS ALMOST EMPTY. I parked the pickup under a sign marked "University of Manitoba, St. Philip's College, Reserved Parking Only" and walked across the muddy lot past the suspicious parking-lot attendant. The dirty camper truck with British Columbia plates, the strange woman with a briefcase demanded his close scrutiny. I ignored him.

Safely through the big double doors and into the standard 1950s interior of the college, I glanced at a board that told me that Dr. J.B. Millwell's office was on the third floor of the New Wing. Nothing indicated how to get to the New Wing; the building I was in had only two stories. I broke into a very private conversation between two students and was told, in tones of surprise at my ignorance, that the New Wing was through the hall to the left. Finally, after losing myself at least twice, I found the third floor of the New Wing and walked slowly past the faculty lounge to a door marked "Linguistics". A small office. two desks, a woman behind a typewriter, and a number of doors, one of which was labeled "Professor James B. Millwell".

"Come in," came the response to my knock.

"Professor Millwell? I'm Helen Keremos. You sent for me."

A second of disorientation and ....

"Oh, Mrs .... *Ms*. Keremos." He pronounced the "Mizz" carefully, quotation marks in his voice. "I didn't expect you so soon; hope you had a good trip. Did you fly?" Giving himself time, getting himself together, deciding how to handle me.

"I drove. I usually do."

Small talk is useful. I sat down, put my superfluous brief-case on the floor, looked at him, the books, the room. To be honest, he was a surprise. I had not expected anyone so bland, so without style. Most university professors try hard to project some image: hip or trendy, scholarly, radical, eccentric, or just-one-of-the-guys. If only as a defense to impress their students.

This dude was none of these, not much of anything. Well-barbered head and face, neat tweed jacket, non-descript shirt and tie, conservative glasses, manicured nails. His office, furnished in standard college chairs, desk and shelves complete with books, files in well-controlled disarray, gave nothing away. There were no family photos, no mementos, no pipe. Careful, very careful, that was the word for Millwell.

"You drove! From Vancouver? Well, it's the time of year for it. Through Banff?" he asked, for something to say.

"No, Crowsnest Pass." As if it mattered. He was having trouble getting to the point. I decided to help out.

"You sent me a check. You have a job for me. What's it about?"

"My son. I want you to find him."

He took out an envelope from a desk drawer and slowly extracted a three-by-five snapshot. Head and shoulders of a young man, thin, blond, handsome in an unfinished, boyish way, good features, longish, well-cared-for hair, work shirt, no glasses.

"His name is Martin. This is the best photo I have of him." Millwell kept talking while I examined the picture.

"He's 18 now, two weeks ago, September 8. Good-looking boy, isn't he? Like his mother. This was taken a year ago; it's a good likeness."

Nerves. So I was getting all this extraneous jive. Not unusual under the circumstances. But we had to get on with it.

"How long has he been gone, how did he disappear?"

"Last June .... yes, June. He went to Toronto with a couple of friends. He was through high school, graduated, you know. Good student. But his interest was guitar: folk, country, that kind of thing, you know. So he went to this festival in Toronto. Mariposa Music Festival it's called. Perhaps you've heard of it?"

"Yes, I've heard of it. Go on. How did he travel and with whom?"

"These two boys. Friends of his. I don't know much about them. One of them had a car, or use of a car. His name is Andrew

Walec. I've talked to his father. The other was named Oscar. That's all I know. They went together. Then I received a card from Martin from Toronto saying they had arrived."

"Nothing since?"

"No."

"Mr. Millwell. It's now the end of September. You sent for me a week ago. How come you waited almost three months? Did you make any effort to trace your son, to find out what happened to him? What about the other two boys? Are they back? Do you know?" I threw questions at him.

"Oh, I tried. I talked to Andrew's father, Mr. Walec. His son had come back as scheduled at the end of June. In August he left to work in British Columbia; lumbering or tree planting I believe. Mr. Walec knew nothing about Martin, couldn't tell me whether they had come back together or not. And could not, or would not, tell me how to reach Andrew. His English is poor, you know. These people are hard to pin down. Anyway, he told me Andrew is in the bush somewhere. Said he would let me know when his son got in touch."

"How about Oscar?" I asked.

"I didn't know his last name. How could I find him?"

"And that's all you did to find your son? You didn't communicate with the Ontario provincial police, Missing Persons in Toronto? No one else in your family or any of your friends have heard from him?"

"No. No. I didn't call in the police. You see, well, it's difficult. His mother lives in Ontario. We're separated, you know. At first I thought Martin had gone to see her, perhaps decided to stay, and .... and just forgot to let me know. But then on his birthday Katherine called, that's my wife, my ex-wife I mean to say, asking to speak to him, wish him happy birthday, you know. It was clear he was not with her and she thought he was here. That's why it took me so long."

He had this part of his story down pat. There was one more question he had to expect to be asked.

"Why call me, Mr. Millwell? All the way from Vancouver to

find your son last heard from in Ontario?"

Quickly, nervously he explained.

"I didn't know who to get in Winnipeg or Toronto. How does one know these things? Then a friend of mine, a lawyer in Vancouver, recommended you. Said you specialized in finding people, tracing missing persons, recovering stolen goods, and that type of thing. Recommended you very highly. So naturally ...."

"Yes, all right. Now I want to know as much as you can tell me about Martin, his friends, interests, family, and so on."

It took another hour. Martin emerged as a good, but not outstanding student, not interested in linguistics or higher education but only in folksinging, his guitar. He had a friend named Sue Packer — Millwell spoke her name with reserve — a sociology major at the university. Drugs, booze? No, not as far as Millwell knew. But then he did not know much about his son, except the most superficial things. The boy had been very much on his own since his mother left Winnipeg. Millwell was a busy man, did not understand or share Martin's life. Martin was quiet, gave no trouble, and had never disappeared before. If he stayed out nights it would be at a folk club, listening or playing. Previous summers he had gone to camp; he liked canoeing and was an outstanding swimmer. He wanted to have this summer to himself before deciding on college or a job. His father thought that reasonable and did not object. No close family, other than his mother, that Martin was likely to contact. Sue Packer? Perhaps she might know something, but in Millwell's opinion she was a strange girl so he had not tried to talk to her. It would have been useless, he was convinced. It was clear Packer and Millwell did not get along. Anyone else? No one he could think of. Neighbors? Hardly. School buddies, other folksingers? Again, perhaps, but no name came to mind.

No word since June, except for a postcard, which he had not kept. It had been just the regular "Arrived safely, having wonderful time." No address, no hint of plans. Martin's mother, Katherine Payne, was an artist, now living with another artist, a potter named Donald McPherson near Toronto. The Millwell marriage had never been great. Katherine had left when Martin was 12. Big enough not to need a mother.

"She was not much of a mother anyway. Too selfish — like most artists, you know."

Millwell's tone implied that Martin was better off without her influence. But mother and son had been close. Millwell found this hard to accept.

And so it went .... pages of notes, mostly useless, but you never can tell at this stage what will prove relevant. So I let him rap on and on. At last Millwell turned himself off and offered me coffee. It was almost 5 P.M.

"I will have my girl get it; it's no trouble," he said.

His "girl" was the woman in the outer office. Certainly full-grown and with better things to do than serve us coffee.

"No thanks, I can get it myself on the way out."

"Will you help me?" Millwell asked.

"Mr. Millwell, I'll do what I can. You understand Martin is of age and cannot be made to come back if he chooses not to."

"Of course, there is no question of that. I am just worried about him and want to know where he is and what happened."

"As long as that's understood. I'll be in touch. The check you sent will serve as retainer."

"What are you going to do? How will you go about it?"

"Talk to people, first here, then in Toronto; what else?"

"Well, let me know the minute you learn anything. I'm very anxious, you know .... It may not show, but ...."

"Naturally."

2

CROSSING THE PARKING LOT AGAIN on the way back to the truck I spotted the woman from the outer office of the Department of Linguistics getting into a Honda Civic. A child's toy fell out as she opened the door. I walked over, picked it up, and looked at her. And liked her.

"I'm Helen Keremos. I saw you in Professor Millwell's office."

It's hard to resist giving your name when someone has just given you theirs. It worked.

"I'm Phyllis Erenberg. Yes, I work there. As a secretary," she added quickly, not wanting to be mistaken for one of the ruling classes. "You were in talking to Millwell." Just "Millwell", no "Professor".

"Yes. About Martin."

"He's disappeared, hasn't he? Millwell never said, but it's pretty obvious."

"I've been hired to find him. Any idea of why he would decide to drop out of sight? Any reasons you can think of?"

"Not like that, no. He was a considerate boy. I'm sure he would have let his father know he was all right if he had meant to stay away. And especially his mother."

"Oh, you know Katherine Payne?"

"For your information Katherine Payne is a well known sculptor. And yes, of course I know her. I have worked here for four years, and before that .... I was a faculty wife, and before that a student here."

"And now you're one of the working class," I smiled. And received a smile in return. We were tuned in.

"Right. Now I make coffee and type letters for the Millwells of this world. A wife is just a husband away from welfare. I was lucky to get this job."

A debatable point, but at least she was not sorry for herself. The subject was due to be dropped.

"So you knew Martin. What's he like?"

"A nice boy, a very nice boy. Good student, good athlete, popular ...."

"Yes, yes, I know all that. I want the sort of things that *don't* get into a high-school yearbook. Like .... what does he feel strongly about? What turned him on? Money, dope, sex? You know what I mean. How about radical politics? Was he unstable, had a bad temper, been in trouble with the law? Was he into ESP, Transcendental Meditation? Varieties of Buddhism? Chanting? Alternatives to Alienation? A Jesus freak? Some other mind fucks? Was he a vegetarian, a back-to-the-earth freak? Was he into therapy: Gestalt, Primal? How about I Ching, astronomy, tarot? Those are the kind of things I want to know. Can you help?"

"No. You better talk to Sue Packer. She knew him as well as anyone." She had turned off quite abruptly. Suddenly she was in a hurry. "Please excuse me but I must get away. My children go to after-school care. I must pick them up. Before six." It was only 5:15 but I let her go. She had her reasons for cutting our conversation short.

"Just one more queston: have you ever heard of a friend of Martin's named Oscar?"

"Oscar? Oscar who? No, I haven't. Now really, I must go. Good luck." Now she really was in a hurry.

I found Sue Packer running a printer in the basement office of an off-campus radical newspaper. Before I reached her I had found out that she was a top student and a "shit disturber". Went in for causes I was told, in and out of season. Which meant the causes were not of the popular liberal variety. She was described as a political heavy, a leader among the small number of active Winnipeg student radicals. None of which was my business and none of which tied in with Martin and his guitar. But she would talk to me. In fact she was not a bit nervous or flustered. Experience in being interviewed by hostiles, no doubt. Not that I was hostile, but she was not to know that.

"Sue, I want to know about Martin. Why did he split? He's over 18; he doesn't have to come back, just let his folks know he is okay. What about it?"

"Millwell hired you, right? Why? It doesn't make sense."

Bright woman. It did *not* make sense; Millwell's explanation was weak indeed. Hiring a woman investigator from Vancouver to find a young man in Toronto just did not scan. And a thousand-dollar retainer when he could have had an agency in Toronto do a little checking for a couple of hundred.

I told her I quite agreed, and no, I did not know why me. But I was hired, paid, and working. Could she help me? Would she?

She turned off the machine at the end of the run.

"About Martin? Martin was a really fine person. Do you understand? No bullshit about him. Music was his life, he wanted to play and that's all he wanted. So he went to Toronto, to Mariposa. He thought he might make contacts there, get help, gigs, make a living doing what he most wanted in the world. That's all I know."

"Oh, come on! You were friends, lovers? Right? You're a smart, committed woman. Political, that's obvious. What about him? How did he fit into your life and you into his? Why bother talking to me if you don't intend to say anything?"

"It's hard to talk about him. Martin was a good friend, possibly my only male friend. You know men — including men in the Left? They use people, especially women. They need and demand constant support, attention. Martin was a relief from all that I have to put up with here, and on campus. He was truly human, open, non-manipulative, non-sexist. He agreed with what I was doing but could not get involved because he was one of those who believe that Art is apolitical. We had many arguments about that. He thought he could escape through music. It's nonsense, of course. Everything is political. So-called personal solutions amount to a tacit support of the system. But we were friends, lovers sometimes. Nothing heavy, but trusting and loving. What more can I tell you? He was a good man."

"'Was'?"

"I haven't heard from him in two months, more like three in fact. Yes, I have to believe he's dead. Or very sick. There's no other explanation."

"Not necessarily. He could have gotten into something he didn't want you to know about. And did not want to destroy your image of him. Pride, perhaps. He is young, after all. It's possible, or have you thought of that?"

"Yes it's occurred to me. I don't believe it."

"What about Oscar? Who is he?"

"Oscar? Who told you about Oscar?" Suddenly she was concerned.

"Martin's father."

"Oh, that doesn't mean anything."

And that was that. I promised to let her know when I found out anything. As I left she turned back to the machine, to the piles of colored leaflets she was printing, her movements sure and economical. Fully in control. An impressive woman.

That night I called Toronto. I lived and worked there for a while not so long ago and even though I have been back on the West Coast for the last six years, I still have contacts, friends. It would speed things up to have some checking done with the cops, the Mariposa office, various booking agencies, to see whether anyone had heard of Martin Millwell. It would take me three days to get there myself.

I also talked to Mr. Walec, whose English was quite adequate. His son had come back from Toronto alone — or at least, without Martin. Also, Mr. Walec had never heard of Oscar and was sure that Andrew and Martin had left Winnipeg without a companion. He gave me Andrew's address, care of General Delivery in a small town in the B.C. interior. I sat down in the camper that night and wrote a letter full of questions, giving a Toronto return address. The mysterious Oscar was beginning to bug me. I hoped Andrew would have some answers.

3

LEAVING BIRD'S HILL PROVINCIAL CAMPGROUND at six the next morning, I picked up the Trans-Canada and settled down to the 1,500-mile trip east. I enjoy these long drives alone over almost traffic-free highways. The feeling of apartness is exhilarating. I do my best thinking then.

Going over the story from Millwell, Erenberg, Packer, Walec. Who was Oscar? Did Millwell make him up? If so, why? More probably Martin had lied about there being a third passenger to Toronto. Again, why? There did not appear to be any point to it. And why was I hired? Millwell did not strike me as someone who did unconventional things. Hiring a woman detective was out of character and one from Vancouver was absurd. Both Erenberg and Packer had picked up on this inconsistency.

I gave up on that and mulled over Packer. The situation there was more understandable and possibly significant. I could see how someone like Sue would get into a man like Martin, and vice-versa. But I was sure there was something she had not told me, something she preferred to keep hidden. Her interest when I mentioned Oscar. Oscar again. Damn!

Traveling eastward from Winnipeg, the Shield creeps up on you before it hits you in the teeth. Starting flat and open, the landscape first closes in with trees, then buckles and folds. The Ontario border arrives too soon from Winnipeg; the space does not fit the time. East begins two days west of Toronto. It's absurd and confusing but it's true. What does it is the Shield. Lake-of-the-Woods, North-of-Superior, Georgian Bay, Muskoka: mile after mile of crushing, total integrated familiarity.

For a day or two there is little but the trucks, rocks, trees, lakes — and me. It's a joy wheeling the green half-ton over empty stretches of solid Ontario highway, interspersed with clumps of traffic.

In Thunder Bay I stop for a booze-up with an old friend. After that the gorgeous Lake Superior road passes like a dream. Raise the temperature 10 degrees Fahrenheit and these beaches and hills wold be crawling with tourists. I bless our climate.

It's after Labour Day, so camping is free in Lake Superior Provincial Park. It gets my business. By now I have quit thinking about the Millwell job; it's a job after all, and will follow its own logic.

There is now a bypass at Sudbury. Saves time and gas, with just a glimpse of INCO stacks and polluted landscape. Through the cottage country traffic thickens. Soon, I hit the six-lane south to Toronto, then the multi-lane 401 Highway, and finally the Don Valley Parkway through the heart of the city. It's still light when I stop at a small house in the Beaches district of Toronto.

Toronto is a big city. It has it all. Stuffy business downtown, rowdy mid-town, deadly middle-class suburbs, pleasant mixed neighborhoods of old homes with large yards and neat working-class houses. The Beaches is like that. It is essentially an old Anglo area: people who have lived here for generations with an influx of more adventurous migrants. Unlike the rest of Toronto, it faces the lake and lives by and through the strip of beach on its southern edge.

Lake Ontario is not the Pacific, and Alex's house is far removed from my second-floor walkup in Vancouver's Chinatown, just a bottle throw away from the sleaze of Hastings and Main. But it's as near to a home as I have had since leaving my father's house in San Diego many years ago. Anyway, it brings back memories of my stint in Toronto in the sixties.

Impatient, I park and rattle the front door hoping Alex is in. She is. Great!

4

ALEX EDWARDS IS A FREELANCE RESEARCHER, as well as production assistant and what-have-you for the CBC. She knows everyone, can find out everything and arrange anything.

It was a fine reunion. We sat up most of the night drinking beer. Rapping about this and that and going over the Millwell case.

"Look, this is all I've been able to get you, just a once-over. Here is who has *not* heard of Martin Millwell: the CBC, CTV, the Folklore Center, Riverboat, one guy in the Mariposa office. I think you'll have to check that one again: someone else might be more co-operative. As for the booking agencies, I've called the top eight — zilch! So take it from there, Toronto cops have never heard of him, so they say, but who knows? Can't get the time of day from that lot."

"That's a start, all negative, but a start. Now. How about Katherine Payne? Anything on her or her old man McPherson."

"Sure. Look, she's one of our top sculptors. Lives on a farm in the Caledon Hills. Works all the time, never see her in town. McPherson belongs to the Guild of Potters, a good run-of-the-mill craftsman, not in her class, but sound. He's around, has to peddle his stuff. Drinks. Teaches a class at the Free Art School. You can probably catch him there."

"Anything on Oscar?"

"Oscar, Oscar! Animal, vegetable, or mineral? Look, you have to give me more than just 'Oscar'."

Alex hates to be stumped. I admitted the name "Oscar" was not much to go on and promised to get her what I could, if I could.

"Alex, you checked all those places by phone, right? How sure can we be that there is nothing to be gotten out of them?"

"As far as their records are concerned, I'm pretty sure. I know the female office slaves at the CBC and CTV and most of the agencies. They really checked for me. But the others .... The guy at the Mariposa office couldn't be bothered. And there is Fiddlers Green, and Harbourfront, Bohemian Embassy, and a dozen others. They should be hit in person. The cops? You know the cops. It's anybody's guess what they know and what they'll tell a mere citizen. Listen, perhaps he was using another name? You have a photo?"

"Sure I have a photo. I'll flash it around, but I doubt he would be using a stage name. Doesn't fit with what I know about him."

"Oh? What do you know about him, really? Or is there something you haven't told me?"

"No. It's just instinct, hunch."

"Instinct, bullshit. Don't give me that. I'm not sure how you make a living detecting, but I bet it's not by instinct or hunches."

"Don't knock it. Sometimes it's all I have. And don't be so coy about 'detecting'. You know damn well how it's done. What about all those 'industrial espionage' capers we did together? Now you're all respectable and can call it 'research' or 'data search' but the principle is the same. You just give your hunch a different, more scientific handle, like 'probability based on informed experience'. A hunch by any other name."

"Nuts."

Alex has no problems communicating.

"That industrial stuff was different. We were after specific information and we were well briefed. We knew what to look for and where. But this! It's all nebulous. And all those people! There's no center, no real data. Give me real research every time. I like to know what I know and what I have to find out."

"Good enough. If all you want to do is 'data search', there's a lot of that too. I'll do my usual prowling and confronting people and you can do the backroom stuff. Suits me."

"Suits me too. Okay. You do the job your way and just tell me what hard facts you need. It's your riff. How about my pay? By the hour?"

"Oh, you want to be just hired help? I thought maybe after expenses we could split the fee down the middle, but I'm easy.

You want a wage, okay. What do you charge per hour?"

"Hell, no. I'll take half the fee, whatever that turns out to be."

"It won't be much after expenses, unless we find some side gravy."

"Unless *you* find it, you mean. Okay, that's a deal. Oh, man, it's just like old times! I missed you, you know, you and your funny businesses. It's been a dull life mostly since you went back west."

"Nuts."

It was my turn to be succinct. "Nothing about you or your life has ever been dull, but thanks for the compliment. I missed you too."

So we did the old times trip, too tired to go to bed until early morning.

5

NEXT TWO DAYS I DID THE ROUNDS — clubs, agencies, bars, health-food stores, record companies. "Martin Millwell?" A glance at the photo. No. "At Mariposa? Look, there were thousands. All look alike, all think they can out-do Ian Tyson or Neil Young or Hank Snow or whoever they're currently into. Who can tell them apart?"

"Don't any of them make it, at least get some gigs?"

"I guess, but this one I ain't seen."

So it went for two full days and nights. The third day I called at the Free Art School, a shabby house in the southern, less-improved part of Cabbagetown. Pottery room was in the basement. It was a busy place with a number of ill-assorted individuals milling about. Don McPherson was due to give a class.

"You're looking for Don? Should be here any time, unless he stopped off at the Winchester for a couple."

"Likes his beer, eh?"

"No more than most. What's it to you? You a dry or something?"

Defensive. Don obviously a favorite here. Serious young woman in a dirty smock listening to this exchange, hands in pockets, dark eyes steady on my face. Finally she spoke up.

"Who are you? What do you want with Don?"

"I'm looking for Martin Millwell. Know him?"

"Never heard of him. What's he got to do with Don?"

"Martin's mother is Katherine Payne. That mean anything to you?"

"Katherine's son? You're kidding!" Very interested and incredulous.

"You didn't know Katherine had a son? Well, I guess there was no reason for Don to tell you. Anyway, were any of you around last June? During Mariposa? He was in town, Martin.

Plays the guitar. About 18. Here's his picture. Anyone recognize it?"

"Oh, him. Yeah — two, three months ago I saw him at the Selby with Don. It's a bar. That's all. Didn't know who he was. Left them alone."

Finally a strike.

"When was that? Can you be more specific?"

"Don't know. I've been here all summer and so has Don. At summer school. Early, I think. Early in summer, I mean. June. July. Not recently." That's all I got out of her.

Don McPherson had not shown up and no one was much surprised or upset. They described him to me and I went the rounds of local taverns. Not an elevating experience in that area. Upwardly mobile, trendy young couples have not yet managed to push all of society's discards from this desirable central city location. Taverns were still their strongholds. Since it was early in the day, the clientele was sparse and consisted largely of winos, various dropouts of the type that send shivers down the spines of "respectable" citizens. Not being a respectable citizen it didn't faze me much. I was half full of good Ontario draft when I spotted him at the Avion. He was alone, three empty and one full draft glasses in front of him on the beer-stained table. He had his head in his hands, but it was him. There was no mistaking the description. For some reason I decided on a formal approach.

"Mr. McPherson?"

"Uh?! Yes?"

"My name is Keremos. Here's my card. I would like to talk to you about Martin Millwell, your stepson."

That brought him to his senses. He ignored my card, sat up, and glared.

"He is not my stepson! Whatever gave you that idea? What do you want?"

"Where is he, do you know?"

"Back in Winnipeg as far as I know, or in some folknik joint just about anywhere. He hung around for a couple of weeks as he does each summer and then split. What do you want him for?"

"As he does each summer? You mean he comes to Toronto every summer? I was told he went to camp."

"Yeah, camp. One of these rich kids' camps on Georgian Bay somewhere. Sailing, swimming, orienteering — a battalion of counselors, doctors, analysts, probably maids and footmen for all I know. Shit! But he always visited his mother for a couple of weeks first. At the farm. What's it to you?"

"And he was here again this year?" I asked.

"Yeah. But no camp this time. No, this time he was going to get into the music business. Like showbiz. Write songs. Not bad if you like that sort of thing. Why the interest?"

"Do you remember when you saw him last and the circumstances?"

"Last? Well, it wasn't at the farm. Must have been in town. Yeah, with that new agent of his, he introduced us, I don't know why. I don't know or care anything about that business. But Martin always wanted us to be buddies. Buddies."

"What was the agent's name, please try to remember."

"Nate something — Ottoway, Otoman, who knows. Something pretty unlikely. Tough-looking character, not Martin's kind I would have thought. Martin told me he was staying at the Colonnade in Nate's apartment. Must be doing okay to afford a pad there."

McPherson was getting interested, sobering up. His eyes focused on me, gray, intelligent, too old for his face. Becoming aware he was being pumped and getting no answers in return.

"Okay. I told you what you wanted to know. Now it's your turn. Who are you, what do you want Martin for, and what's this all about?"

"You're holding my card. Professor Millwell hired me to find Martin, who has not been heard from since June."

He looked at his hand still holding my card as if he had not seen either before.

"Helen Keremos, Private Investigator. Hmm. And a Vancouver

address. You're a long ways from home, Helen. Why would that pompous ass Millwell hire someone from Vancouver? And a woman, at that?"

"Any ideas about that? His check was good — and substantial."

"So you don't know either! Well, well, well. Katherine will be amused. Substantial check, eh? Doesn't sound like dear James. Careful man with his money is James. Well, well, well."

He had forgotten all about Martin in his genuine amusement. Whatever was bothering him was not "dear James". McPherson was getting himself together. He finished his beer, stretched and stood up.

"I have to go and see how my flock is doing. Hey, how did you find me? Someone told you at the FArt? That this is my home away from home?"

"Yeah, they were helpful."

"They are good, you know. Most of them. Too good for me. Good people, good artists. Cover for me, indulge me, treat me like a child in need of loving care."

"And are you? In need of loving care?"

"Isn't everyone? No, I guess not. But many of us are, my vintage. Casualties of the fifties is how I see it."

We were walking out together now, heading for the school. He kept on talking.

"It's too bad. We have the craft, the skill, the knowledge, the training. And don't know what to do with it. Some of these kids; well, they're different. They want to get right to it, to be doing, creating. They take shortcuts, skim off the cream, get bored in a hurry. Makes it tough for them to learn what they need to learn. Frustrates them like all hell. But it's fun being with them. They teach me more than I can teach them, really. And much of what I know, what I've learned in the past is horseshit. They see it and don't let me get away with much. Mind you, they're amazingly naive and ignorant. They make mistakes like you wouldn't believe. Then they come back to old Don and say, 'Hey, man, what did we do wrong? Show us how.' It's not that they won't take direction, exactly. Just that they want what they want without all the bullshit it usually comes with. It's very purifying. Know what I mean?"

"Sure. In my business you have to accept uncertainty as the norm. You can never know for sure in advance. And it doesn't matter. It means that you have to take risks, not be careful like your friend Millwell."

"Right on! You got it. Except he's not my friend."

He was laughing, striding along Gerrard Street, eyes bright, beard flying. A different man from the one I first spotted in the tavern. Suddenly he stopped, grabbed my arm.

"Look here, you must meet Katherine. Come out to the farm. Better call first, see if she wants visitors. Here's the number. Call tonight. We'll rap and split a jug. And you can ask her about Martin. I keep out of these things, that part of her life. But I know she'll be concerned. She and Martin are pretty close. Do come. Okay?"

"I was just about to invite myself. Yes, I must see Katherine. I'll try for tonight."

"It's a deal. Oh, here we are. 'Bye, now."

"Bye, and thanks."

"*De nada*," he said, proving that like every potter he had been to Mexico.

He marched off whistling to his flock.

I had seen metamorphoses like that before: alcoholics can be quick-change artists. He was not so far gone that he could stop himself from trying to impress. I was a woman, sympathetic; I had reacted well to him. The high would probably carry him through the day and perhaps into the evening, which was all to the good if I was going to pay them a visit at the farm.

It would not be hard to find the Nate O-something dude unless he was a complete phony. I went looking for a phone booth to get Alex onto him at once.

6

THE ROAD TO CALEDON passes through Toronto's expensive exurbia. Five-and ten-acre ranchettes, country houses, ski chalets dot the landscape, interspersed with tightly fenced estates, race-horse farms, and other examples of conspicuous affluence. Split-rail fences, well-fed children on well-fed ponies, polite service people, beautifully restored old barns, antique stores in perfect taste. Even all that could not quite spoil the rich Ontario fall landscape, the texture of rough, home-spun tweed. Homeward-bound traffic thinned out and it was getting dark when the mobile phone buzzed. It had to be Alex with word on Nate O. It was.

"Glad I got you before you arrived at Paynes'. Your Mr. O is quite a lad. His name is Nathaniel Ottoline, or at least that's the only name he is known under. He does indeed live at the Colonnade, and yes, he is an agent of sorts. But from all accounts — and I have had only four hours to turn this up — he turns his hand to other, less salubrious enterprises. Most anything to make a buck. You want it all now or will it wait?"

"Now, all of it. Just let me get off the road."

No matter what you see on TV, it's hard to drive a truck, listen to the phone, and perhaps take notes at the same time. I pulled over, one-handed, and stopped.

"Okay, let's have it from the top."

"Right. Nate Ottoline has been in Toronto eight to 10 years; it's hard to pin down exactly. From somewhere in the Ottawa Valley. First heard from managing a local rock group, which soon died without leaving a trace. One of hundreds. Since then, has done well if you like that sort of thing. You name it, he's been in it. Porno quickies for the stag trade, some Yonge Street strip stuff, after hours clubs. He has an interest in one now, runs a couple of acts for the smaller legit joints, probably peddles a little coke, stuff like that. He knows everyone in the trade, has made some cheapie American commercials with non-union crews, will put together anything you want for a price. All on the fringes of showbiz — music, TV, films. You know the scene. Reputed to swing both ways. He might well have cruised Mariposa for business and or pleasure."

"Nice lad. What else?"

"Well, just impressions. Like I said, I haven't had much time. He's a loner, works solo, no organizational connections I could find. That makes him special and good. Tough and competent, knows his stuff. Could be a handful so be careful."

"Careful?" I laughed. "This is such a 'careful' case it will be a relief to deal with Mr. O. Where will I find him, say tomorrow?"

"I didn't exactly check with his social secretary, but as near as I can figure his schedule, in the A.M. he's either at home or at his 'health' club — The Playdough. You'll have trouble getting in, it's men only. In the P.M. it's harder to say, but he often eats and spends time at that French joint on Avenue Road. You could try there."

"The old Auberge? Anyone who likes it there must be okay some of the time. Is that all you have?"

"Yes, what did you expect? Personally, I think it's pretty good."

"I think it's great, but I wouldn't want to repeat that before witnesses. Thanks."

"Nice to be appreciated. Will you be home tonight? I may have company, so if you come in late use tact."

"Will do. Have fun. Bye."

So it sure looked as if young Martin had picked himself some heavy company. I wondered what his mother knew about it and how she would react when she found out. The personality of Katherine Payne was dominant in my mind. I had now met her ex-husband James and current housemate Don McPherson. Also, I had heard the awe in the voices of Erenbeg and the nameless young woman at the FArt. Even Alex had sounded impressed — and she does not impress easily. The newly discovered figure of Nate Ottoline was fading from my imagination as I drew closer to the Payne/McPherson farm.

This turned out to consist of a shabby clapboard farmhouse, surrounded by a disreputable barn and tackle sheds, old trees and weeds. The mailbox just said "McPherson". Payne obviously liked her anonymity. A windbreak of trees lined the short drive that led up to the house from the gravelled concession road. I parked the pickup out of the way and walked to the back door; no one uses the front in setups like this. McPherson opened the door almost before I reached it; a dog rushed out between his legs, barking. McPherson had a bottle of beer in one hand; he pulled me in with the other.

"Come in, come in. Katherine is real anxious to meet you. Told her all about our conversation at the good old Avion. Yes, yes, glad you could come tonight. Have a beer."

It was not a question. I accepted a bottle. The house was the regular center-plan Ontario farmhouse, stairs leading directly up from in front of the unused main door, the large kitchen on the left, the 'good' parlor on the right, and two everyday rooms on the flip side.

Katherine came into the kitchen, hand outstretched, just as McPherson was opening my beer. That was unusual right there: women seldom shake hands with each other in the Anglo culture. Tall, thin, very blond, Nordic, with rather prominent blue eyes, strong uneven teeth, a sprinkling of freckles. The likeness to Martin was evident, but his picture had him better-looking than she was. She had on a Mexican shirt-smock over army pants. Her hands were dirty; she did not apologize or comment on her appearance.

"Right. Now that you're here we'll eat soon. And then you can tell me about Martin." This seemed a strange way to start. Katherine's lack of interest or concern did not ring true at all.

"I was hoping you could tell me," I said.

"Yes, I know. But right now I'm starving. Don, how's supper?"

"Katherine sometimes forgets to eat at noon. So do I but then

I drink to make up for it."

McPherson, bottle in hand, smiling, watching Katherine Payne and I get acquainted. He was enjoying it. I was not sure precisely why. Payne ignored the second part of the comment.

"I love good food but hate to break into concentrated work just to have a snack. Especially when I have to make it myself. Takes me hours to get back into my work afterwards." She went on. "It's really my turn to make supper tonight but Don will see to it while you and I talk. Perhaps you would like to see my studio?"

"Very much."

"Grab your drink and let's go."

Payne's studio turned out to be in the barn, although the whole house was full of her work, her taste, her *persona*. She created sculpture unlike any I had ever seen. It was small in scale, rough-textured, and utterly unexpected in shape and meaning. Every piece started out looking one way and became something else the longer one looked at it. Odd angular shapes haunted the imagination like the accidental images of driftwood. I had trouble coming to terms with the reality of Katherins's work, no less then with that of the artist herself. The impression was stunning.

We were sitting on wooden stools in her studio when she brought us back to Martin.

"What did James tell you about Martin? How did he come to hire you?"

I described my talk with Millwell in some detail, mentioned encounters with Erenberg and Packer. For the time being no word on Ottoline. She listened attentively, nodding her head in a couple of places.

"Yes, I see. Well, for starters I think I can tell you who Oscar might be. He lives right next door. Oscar and Martin have been friends for a number of years. They went to the same camp and spent time together every summer while Martin was in Ontario."

"Why then did Millwell tell me they traveled down from

Winnipeg together and why did everyone pretend they didn't know who Oscar was?"

"Erenberg might not have known. Oscar has never been to Winnipeg. And as for my ex- .... James Millwell is the most roundabout person I know. He threw in Oscar to be sure you checked into his connection with Martin, but he could not bring himself to say directly that he suspected Oscar was somehow involved with Martin's disappearance. At least that's my explanation. Yes, the whole situation is very much in character. James is incapable of being out front about anything. Anything, believe me. His mind is so convoluted he doublecrosses himself. But he is not stupid. If he connected Martin with Oscar, then there is something in it."

"And do you agree?"

"Now I think about it, yes. I'll get Don to tell you more about our neighbours later. Now let's get to what happened."

"That's what I'm here for. But just one more thing about James. Would his 'character' explain why he hired me rather than someone more likely?"

"Yes, yes, it all fits. Just one more of his ways of being careful, yes."

"Okay, let's leave it at that. Now, what happened this summer?"

"This is all I can tell you: Martin arrived this June with Andy Walec. They spent a night here and then went on to Toronto Island for the three-day Mariposa Folk Festival. I didn't go this year. I used to go regularly but now so much *gemutlich* just bores me. It was different years ago; Mariposa had guts then. Now it's more like a dish of warm milk, except for all the nasty macho crap. Anyway, there are few highs or lows, just the old folknik crowd on a nostalgia trip and kids sitting on the grass smoking up. It's more peaceful than a Baptist picnic and about as exciting or relevant. Three days of it is about two-and-a-half too many. But the boys were into all that so they went. I think Oscar was there too. About a week later Martin called, very excited. He said he had met an agent who would take him on, get him work. I was happy for him but sceptical. Don met this agent, so-called, and was impressed — but not necessarily in a positive way. That was, oh, perhaps early July. Since then, nothing from Martin. I assumed that the deal, whatever it was, had fallen through and he had gone back to Winnipeg with his tail between his legs. I didn't want to intrude or hurt his pride, so I left it at that. Then I phoned on his birthday. James was evasive, said only that Martin was not home, which was true but misleading. Then the next thing I knew he called back to tell me Martin had never returned and that he had hired you to find him."

"All right. You are asking me to believe that Millwell purposely misled me, then that Martin would have gone back to Winnipeg without saying goodbye, without even calling you, and that you thought nothing of it. It does not ring right. And then there is this Oscar angle. Everybody picks up on it but no one will tell me anything. How come?"

"I'm sorry if you don't believe me, but that's the way it was. And I thought I explained about James. And Oscar. Don had better tell you about that scene. He and Henry Borg, Oscar's father, went to school together."

"Old school chums, eh? How's that relevant to Martin's Oscar?"

"I'm not sure exactly, but Henry is very relevant to Oscar, so perhaps ...."

"And what is that supposed to mean? You have a nerve calling Millwell indirect. Do you know what happened to Martin? Do you want to know?"

"No, I don't know what happened to him .... And I'm not sure I want to know. Does that answer you?"

"You think he's dead."

"I don't know what to think, but he must be, or else we would have heard from him, wherever he was. He would not worry his father and me like this. He wasn't that kind of person."

"That's what Sue Packer said. Do you know her?"

"Sue Packer. I never met her, but I know of her. Martin often talked about her. She did not approve of me. I stay out of politics and all movements. I'm an artist. Sue thought I influenced Martin to be apolitical."

"And did you?"

"I guess so. By example, mostly, not by proselytizing. Martin and I always understood and respected each other. We are not like mother and son in that respect, but more like two adults with some 20 years difference in age. It's not insurmountable. If he wanted to be involved like Sue, that would have been fine with me. But he did not. He is not a public person."

"Yes, yes and you would never get involved in anything if you could help it."

"Perceptive of you. Quite right. I want to live and work here, make enough to survive simply with just an occasional trip to Mexico or the Canaries. I can't change the world and don't intend to break my heart trying. My work is all I have and all I want."

"And now you believe your son is dead. And you are not pre-pared to do anything about that either."

"Surely that is a different issue. If he is dead, there is in fact nothing that can be done."

"Only to find out what happened. How and why. Anyway, we can't be sure he's dead."

"That's why I'm glad you're here and you are who you are. I think you'll find Martin, dead or alive. I'll help all I can."

Suddenly a loud holler from across the yard.

"Come and get it! Food's on the table." Don McPherson's breezy voice easily penetrated the ancient barnboard and new insulation. A second later he surged into the studio followed by a large barking dog, which proceeded to slobber all over, almost knocking me off the stool. My private audience with Katherine Payne was over, apparently to her relief.

"Great. Let's eat." She was up and out. Don and I and the large dog followed obediently.

We ate in the bright, rather messy kitchen, Don jumping up occasionally to get more beer or serve seconds of a nondescript health-food casserole and a salad. Katherine ate quickly without enjoyment. Her face was gloomy.

"Don, Helen wants to know about Oscar. I told her you are the expert on the Borgs, father and son."

"Ah, we are back to the subject we discussed this afternoon. One of my favorites, as you have no doubt gathered." Don was immediately in full spate, picking his phrases with evident pleasure. "Henry and I were both good middle-class Ontario boys, just too young for the war. That's the Second World War. We went to Western, the University of Western Ontario in London, the heart of conservative mediocrity. London, Ontario, in the fifties, famous in song and story! Anyway, we partied together, played football, drank too much, and chased the local female talent. We were friends and buddies together, we and a whole post-war generation."

Katherine interrupted. "Never mind editorializing, get on with it."

"Sorry. Katherine has heard it all before, but perhaps you will find the background interesting. So. The difference between Henry and I was that he was in Business Administration, a sort of pale copy of Harvard School of Business, and he graduated. While I .... Well let's just say I left 'under a cloud', went to Toronto to the Ontario College of Art, and hence to my glorious career making pots. Henry went into business as was expected and, as was expected, did well. He is currently Vice-President Marketing of a large shoe manufacturing concern, which is of course part of an international conglomerate. What else? He is very, very successful and proud of it. Having acquired all the necessary accoutrements of wife, two children, and a large house in town, he decided to join the executive drive to exurbia and become a gentleman farmer. Let me assure you that Henry is neither — a gentleman or a farmer, I mean. Unfortunately, he is our neighbor and thinks it's A-Okay to have faintly disreputable 'artistic' people like us to impress with his possessions. And our doings make fine cocktail talk at the Granite Club and around the boardroom table. Since you want to know about Oscar, it's not irrelevant (with an arch look at Katherine) that his father is a living fossil of the fifties. The only impression any new idea has made on Henry's lobotomized brain since then is as a handy peg on which to hang a marketing or advertising campaign. That's really the only way that he perceives the changes and ideas of this era. They are all fads or gimmicks to use against poor consumers. No wonder he's successful. You should see what he does with women's liberation! Or maybe you shouldn't — it's sickening."

"Get to the point," Katherine said, sighing.

"I am, I am, give me time. Well, you can imagine his attitude to his children. *His* children, note: his daughter Veronica, being female, was merely expected to be pretty, charming, and to marry well. She did not. To get away from home she got pregnant at 16, married the guy, who was a local nobody, and now lives in Leaside somewhere. Her husband drives an ice-cream truck. That leaves Oscar, the male and naturally the apple of his father's eye, to coin a phrase."

At this point Don paused to get a fresh bottle of beer. Katherine sat still, watching him silently. He continued.

"Oscar is perfect. He is 6'2", 185 pounds of utterly malleable flesh. Daddy knows best about everything. So Oscar is being carefully groomed to be an 18-year-old throwback to the fifties. He is a superjock in engineering at U. of T. Daddy thinks business schools are too intellectual these days. Daddy wanted him to go to Queen's engineering — they make better jocks — but Kingston is too far. He lives in a high-class residence full of superstuds, belongs to the engineering frat, plays football, college hockey, keeps fit with squash. The only books he's allowed to read are on his course, plus Playboy, and even that's suspect since it's not all pictures."

"How on earth did this Neanderthal and Martin ever become friends?" I interrupted.

"Good question, good question. Affluence, possessions, what else? The Borgs have a swimming pool on their tax-deductible 'farm'. Martin loves swimming; the two boys have that in common. And they went to this posh camp together for what, four years, was it Katherine?" He did not wait for her answer. "I can understand dear James wanting the best snob nob for his boy but why you let him get away with it is a mystery."

"No mystery. One camp seemed very like another to me, so when Martin said he wanted to go there with Oscar, there was no reason to prevent him," Katherine answered calmly.

"Well, anyway. The two boys spent most of the last four summers together, whether at camp or here, at the Borgs' pool, or sailing in Georgian Bay, canoeing. All that outdoor number."

"How about this year? Did they see each other?"

"All I know is that Martin went over there the day he and Andy arrived. When he came back after a swim he said Oscar would be in Toronto during Mariposa. I didn't think Oscar was much interested in folk music but he may have thought any music festival would be a gas and decided to go."

"How about Henry? Would he not disapprove of Martin and music as companions for Oscar?"

This time Katherine answered. "Yes and no. You mustn't take everything Don says as gospel. He does exaggerate. Henry was not against the friendship because Martin is a good athlete. At least he's not a sissy or a dope freak or a radical. That's what Henry has tried to shield Oscar from."

"And succeeded. Certainly, Henry was not overjoyed at Oscar's friendship with Martin. He didn't encourage it but he let Oscar have his own way for once."

"And do you know whether Oscar and Martin spent time together in Toronto in June or July?"

"Have no idea .... Martin didn't mention it and Oscar hasn't been around. If you want to see him, he would be in town. Find him at the engineering residence probably."

"I'll do that. Now Don, I want you to tell me about the last time you saw Martin. At a bar, is that right? With Ottoline, the agent."

"That's right, Ottoline, that was the name. How did you know?"

"I found out. It wasn't hard. I also found out that he's not a very savory character."

"I thought as much. Yet he seemed pleasant enough and genuinely interested in Martin." That's all he seemed able to say on the subject.

Katherine picked up on it. "What do you know about this Ottoline, tell me?"

"All I have is third-hand imformation. Let me check him out personally first and report back. Okay? There's no point getting yourself all worked up over hearsay."

"But what's the hearsay? What are you doing, trying to protect me? You must know that's not necessary. Who and what is Ottoline?"

I had blown this one. Not usually so dumb, usually quite able to tell clients' families only what I wanted them to know, what was good for them to know. But Katherine Payne was not your average family, your everyday mother figure. She wanted to know, and I had to tell her. So I did. Everything Alex had told me. She listened with that concentration I had noticed her capable of before.

"So. It could be worse. At least he really is an agent and in the business Martin was so keen to be a part of. There are bound to be people like that. It could be worse; he could have been an out-and-out fraud."

That was certainly looking at the bright side, considering the circumstances. After all, Martin had last been seen with Ottoline. But if she wanted to take it this way, that was okay with me. Time enough to look unpleasant facts in the face when there was nowhere else to look.

After that I stayed around for another couple of hours, saw more of her work, the home, out-buildings, animals. We talked pleasantly and warmly, but not about Martin. All through this period McPherson was silently getting more and more drunk. At 11:30 I left. Katherine had asked me to stay overnight but

I refused. I wanted to start next day bright and early in Toronto. There were two leads to check out — Oscar Borg and Nate Ottoline, and I was itching to get at them.

7

RATHER THAN BOTHERING ALEX THAT NIGHT — it was late before I got to the city — I crashed at a house I knew near High Park. Next morning I made myself breakfast and was out of the house before any one of the theater group who lived there was up. They were friends of Alex, not mine, and would not miss me.

Just after 9 A.M. I was fighting my way through crowds of students going to class at the U. of T.'s main downtown campus. A check at the School of Engineering got me Oscar Borg's address — a room in an old but elegant house on Huron Street. It was owned by his fraternity and had all the characteristics associated with well-established frats. Large living room dominated by a thousand dollars' worth of color TV, shabby armchairs, a coke machine, an enormous worn oriental rug probably donated by an affluent alumnus. Well-polished floor testified to the existence of an army of hired cleaners who had not yet been in that day to pick up the previous night's accumulation of books, dirty ashtrays, socks, empty pizza boxes, and girly magazines scattered throughout the empty public rooms on the ground floor. In the kitchen at the back, a very young-looking man was having a breakfast of tomato juice and stale doughnuts. He grinned at me cheerfully.

"Care to join me? Or would you prefer Eggs Benedict? Wouldn't blame you if you did. Too bad there are none to be had. But my Mama always told me not to face the world on an empty stomach. And there's not even any coffee or O.J. or milk. Brothers cleaned us out last night. Everyone else is still in bed, they won't even get stale doughnuts. Tough. Comes of living in a frat residence. No peace, no food, nobody to tuck you in at night. Change from the old school, you bet. You could have a Bloody Mary; there's some vodka somewhere. Are you a girlfriend, or a mother or a creditor — and whose? This place is such a madhouse. I don't remember seeing you here before.

Hope you didn't come to repossess the TV. No, I guess it's paid for. You're not from the Dean's office, or a liquor inspector. We are not unknown to Toronto's finest. But they would send a man, wouldn't they? No imagination. However ...."

"If you would shut up for a minute, I'll tell you. I'm looking for Oscar Borg."

"Oh, Oscar the football hero. You know I thought all that was long gone but no, not here. I've led such a sheltered life. I'm a freshman, you know. College is quite a surprise. I thought it would be full of intellectuals and radicals; instead, it's full of Oscar Borgs. Nice guy, Oscar. Owns a souped-up Mustang, very generous with it too. I hope it's not serious?"

"Don't kid me, you love it. If you don't, why did you take up engineering?"

"It's a trade, isn't it? Doctors make more, but I don't like sick people so what's left? Accounting? Bah! And it takes too long to get to be a lawyer in this province. And the brainwashing is even worse. So it had to be engineering. But you're right, jocks are fun — so stupid! What do you do for a living?"

"I listen to people run off at the mouth, what else?"

He would not be fazed. "I hope it pays well. It's all nerves, you know. As long as I keep talking I can control myself. Do you think I should take up Primal?"

"I think you should tell me where to find Oscar Borg. Then you can take your own time growing up."

"Growing up? What a drag! It's bad enough that I'll be an engineer, but grown up? No way!"

This witty exchange was interrupted at this point by the arrival of another budding engineer, presumably looking for breakfast. He was much bigger than my current companion, and very much more subdued. He looked morose.

"Hi, Vic. What's to eat?"

"Ah, speak of the young devil himself. May I present Oscar, of the boot-and-shoe Borgs. I'll leave you two together. There's no food. Oscar. None. I must split now. Class, you know. We do attend. It's expected. Bye." He fled, wrapping a long scarf around his head, his brand-new *Roots* squeaking on the tile floor.

Oscar Borg was as advertised, a perfect specimen of young Canadian manhood. Neat blond head on top of an athletic body encased in a U. of T. sweatshirt and well-worn denim pants. He was not all that pleased to have to cope with a strange female at that time of the morning, but as a well-brought-up young man he made the effort.

"That Victor, what a nut! I'm Oscar Borg. Can I do anything for you?"

"Yes, indeed. My name is Helen Keremos and I'm looking for Martin Millwell. Do you know where I might find him?"

"Martin? No. No. He lives in Winnipeg, you know. Why come to me?"

So I told him. Told him just enough: that Martin was missing; that Katherine Payne said he, Oscar, was Martin's friend; that Martin was last seen in Toronto; that I was hired to find him. It all shook him as well it might. He became visibly tense, knuckles locked tight at the back of a kitchen chair, his sentences trailing off.

"I'm sorry I can't help you .... I must go to class, football practice .... I don't know about Martin .... saw him in June I think .... that's all. You must excuse me, I have to go."

Since it was not in my plan to pull him down and sit on his head, at least not this time, I watched him leave still stuttering. I would get around to him again. There was no harm in letting him sweat a while.

8

As soon as the sound of Oscar's size 12s faded into the bowels of the house I went looking for a phone. Alex was home as I expected, just up making brunch. There was mail for me so I invited myself over.

Fresh bagels with Daiters cheese and strong coffee were welcome and excellent but the letter from Andy Walec was superb. I imagined him in a lumber-camp bunkhouse writing this long, detailed, organized letter to someone he didn't know in faraway Toronto. The writing was perfectly controlled and perfectly formed, sentences short, grammatical, and to the point. He imparted information with precision, with a real grasp of the essentials. What I received was a full, detailed account with dates and places of all he knew about Martin, from when they left Winnipeg until his (Andrew's) departure from Toronto 10 days later. He mentioned Ottoline, his afterhours club, The Fly Trap, and Martin's fascination with him; he did a thumbnail on Oscar Borg as Martin's other Toronto friend; Katherine and Don received a brief but incisive comment. I now knew where and when Martin and Ottoline had met, what Andy thought about Henry Borg, and what Martin had said about James Millwell and Sue Packer. An invaluable document, that letter. I promised myself not only to reply, but one of these days to visit young Walec, wherever he was.

Next few hours were spent discussing the case with Alex. Checks had to be run on Henry Borg, Ottoline, and McPherson: their past history, financial status, private lives, and similar, probably irrelevant details. If there was dirt to be dug up, Alex was to find it, whether related to Martin's disappearance or not; I had to have leverage in dealing with these men if I was going to get anywhere. Alex understood this necessity, but had scruples. There was not much I could say to help her. This was not a 'groovy' game where you can enjoy the fun part and then cut out when the work and the dirt begins. We talked it out until she accepted the implication of her involvement in the case. But she drew the line at investigating Katherine Payne.

"Look. No way. She is a woman and an artist, not to mention Martin's mother. I just can't do it. If she has something to hide, I don't want to know about it."

"Okay, okay. We'll leave it at that. Check these three men. Then just to be sure let's find out where James Millwell was in July."

"But he's the father! He wouldn't be involved in Martin's disappearance!"

"Don't be naive. He lied to me, right? Katherine says he's a devious sort of guy. Who knows?"

"I guess you're right. What a nasty business you're in, Helen." There it was again.

"No different from any other, except cleaner than most."

Alex and I are old friends, love and respect each other. The ethical problems of my sort of job were new to her but old hat to me. She had had no trouble handling 'business research'; it was the personal element that fazed her. The distinction she was attempting to make between Borg, Ottoline, and McPherson on the one hand, and Payne and Millwell on the other were easily seen as spurious. On the broader issue she would have to work through the fact that what she, along with other people, did for a living was every bit as 'nasty' as my business. But it's a hard fact to face, so I left her to it.

9

AN AFTERHOURS CLUB DOES NOT HIT ITS STRIDE until after 2 A.M. So it was somewhat surprising that I tracked Ottoline to The Fly Trap that afternoon. It was 5:30 P.M.; the door was closed but a series of sharp knocks brought a breathless young man. Mr. Ottoline was busy, what did I want, who was I? Why don't I come later? He was just doing his job, but sometimes that has to be ignored. I ignored him and pushed in.

The place was empty except for three men who sat at a round table, drinking. Account books filled the spaces between glasses and ashtrays. Three ordinary-looking businessmen, who had obviously just completed some routine book-keeping and were relaxed, socializing. Guess business was good. Only one of the men held my attention. He had followed the short scene at the door with calm curiosity. It was Ottoline all right, but Alex's brief description did not do him justice. He was a long, well-fleshed man in his mid or late thirties. Very dark, bright eyes under heavy brows. Hair cut very, very short in current Yonge street fashion. Also in fashion the casual suit in soft dark blue suede. Forty-dollar patterned shirt and $75 shoes. Just one heavy gold ring. A Patek gold watch. Thin expensive cigar poking out of a full mouth under a well-trimmed moustache. This was going to be fun.

I must have looked pleased; he answered my smile as he looked me over as carefully as I had him.

"It's okay, Ronnie, the lady is determined to see me. Let her."

That was tactful but pointless, since Ronnie could not have stopped me had he tried. Ottoline went on.

"Sit down. What will you have?"

"A beer and half an hour of your time."

"A beer, eh? Do we have beer? I'm not sure. Ronnie, bring the lady a beer."

"No beer, Mr. Ottoline. Perhaps a glass of wine?"

"No wine. Make it a dry martini straight up."

"Right you are. On its way."

Ronnie disappeared into the next room where the bar was.

"And half an hour of your time. Maybe more," I continued.

"That too can be arranged, assuming you have something interesting to say. You don't look like you're selling subscriptions to *Reader's Digest* .... or *The Body Politic* for that matter," Ottoline laughed.

All through this carefully choreographed exchange the other two men at the table looked incuriously in front of them, sipping, inhaling, waiting. Waiting for instructions, for a word from their master that would tell them how to behave, what to do.

"I came about Martin Millwell."

Not a muscle in his face moved, but his next sentence indicated the depth of his interest.

"Ah! Young Martin. Yes, well, I guess we're finished here, gentlemen. Why don't we adjourn this meeting so the lady and I can talk?"

It was an order. Obediently the two shuffled their chairs, finished their drinks, and took themselves off. Meanwhile my drink arrived, I lit up and sat. It took maybe thirty seconds for Ottoline to turn back to me, draw slowly on his cigar, blow smoke at me, and proceed.

"What about Martin Millwell?"

He was serious now; the preliminaries were over. We settled into our chairs, facing each other as if we were about to arm wrestle. For the first time since the beginning of this case I had that exhilarating feeling that comes only when you know all your skill is about to be fully tested. This man lived and succeeded by his wits and guts. He had much to protect and every intention of protecting it. Yet somehow I felt it less necessary to be careful than with the 'nice' people I had met on this case to date. He and I would understand each other soon and well. Whether I got anything useful out of it would depend on whether he decided to trust me; the game we were about to play was merely a way for us to get to know each other. He would not unwittingly fall into any trap. He would gauge me, make his decision based on what would appear to be very little, and that would be that. In his business as in mine, there was no time to be sure. Risk was a part of life; you made snap judgments by feel or instinct or whatever you call it. And you had to be right most of the time or you did not last.

I pushed my card across the table towards him.

"That's me. I was hired to find out what happened to Martin Millwell. He was last seen in your company." Frontal attack.

Ottoline looked at the card without picking it up. And parried.

"A female private-eye! What's a broad doing in that business? And so far from home. Brave for a chick."

A standard male response, but in this case out of character. However, useful to gain time and find out whether I was susceptible to that kind of intimidation.

"No 'broads', 'chicks', or 'little ladies'. You know better. I'm doing a job. A number of people know you knew Martin. It's no secret. He told his mother you were his agent. He stayed at your place. Want to tell me your side of it?"

"My side of it? Are there sides? We met. I liked his work, tried to get him a gig, he couldn't cut it in the big city so he split. That's all."

"Hardly. How long was he with you? Who did you introduce him to? Under what circumstances did he leave, if he left, and when?"

"Questions, questions. He had nowhere to stay in Toronto so I let him use my place until he got settled. Two, three weeks. Then he took off. Haven't heard from him or of him since. Now it's my turn. How did you find me?"

"There are ways. That's what they pay me for. But let me tell you what I think happened. You were cruising Mariposa. Lots of fresh young men. Some even had talent. You picked him up, perhaps just on impulse. But he turned out to be special. You can tell, you've seen enough of the other kind. So you made a mistake; happens to all of us. You two got involved, and that made him realize he was gay. Because he had not known, not really, not then. Just knew he was different. Only woman he ever related to sexually liked him because he was more human than most other males around. He had to acknowledge himself, it was hard: there was his proper, academic father, his beloved mother, his super-straight friends. For a while he fell apart, couldn't do his music bit. Then what happened?"

Pause.

"You know, you're good, very good. But it won't work. Martin knew, you see. He was involved with someone else. It was the world that he couldn't handle; his sexuality was not the problem. The rest is much as you describe it, but ...."

He stopped. A change was indicated, a new play; the struggle was far from over.

"The world is full of handsome boys who think they have talent. In my business I get them crawling all over me. After New York and L.A. this is the biggest draw in North America. Why would I get involved with this Martin from the wilds of Manitoba?"

"Because that's how those things happen. For a poor boy from the Valley you've done okay here. Even lost your accent — almost. But you know how it is, you still remember. Someone helped you when you arrived here. We all come from somewhere. And we outsiders recognize and help each other. Or at least some of us do."

This time the pause was longer. We held eye contact for what seemed a long time.

"So you know I'm from the Valley. Yes. It was a long time ago. But I was poor, never had a suit or three squares a day until I came here. I could have ended as a skid row bum. No money, no friends, no education, and an accent that was harder to live down than if it was a foreign language. No middle-class skills or expectations. It was make it this way or go under. But Martin was different. His background! Shit! He had it all! Solid family connections, education, money, good-boy manners! What is it with these kids, they don't know when they're well off? He could be anything: respectable, rich. This country is designed for men like him. Cops call him 'sir', even in jeans. Helen, what's your full name?''

"Keremos."

"Helen Keremos. Where are you from, Helen?''

"Does it matter? Up from the streets. We know each other. And I too have to make my way. And right now I want to find out what happened to that poor little rich boy, Martin Millwell. Tell me. Who else did he know here, who was he involved with? You said there was someone else. Oscar, maybe?''

"So, you know about that! What are you asking me for? Yes, Oscar, Papa's boy, Oscar. He has tendencies, you see; you know about tendencies?''

"Yes, I know. So what?''

"Okay, for years those two play games with each other at camp, at Papa's swimming pool. Oscar is not dumb, you know. Much smarter than Martin in some ways. Martin still thinks he can have it both ways. That's the difference between them. Martin has guts, but no sense. Oscar is all good middle-class sense, but no guts. Oscar knows what's good for Oscar and that's staying in good with Papa. Dig? Now, Martin wants to connect, wants respectability, wants to do his music thing, wants Mama and Daddy to love him still. Wants it all! No way, you know it, no way. You have to choose. Oscar chose one way, Martin .... well, I don't really know what happened to him.''

"So what happened while you two were together?''

"Okay, okay, if it will help. Well, Martin and Oscar were finally making it, Martin was happy, except that his work was falling apart. I tried to help but they could not deal with where I was, d'you follow? To Oscar I was just a dirty old man, and Martin, well, he was in love and naive and idealistic. He needed me but didn't want to buy into the scene. And there is no other way. It's been easy for him all his life. Why should he have to give up anything, turn into one of those despised queers? He wanted open gay romance, plus success, acceptance, and feeling good about himself all the time. Can you imagine!? Oscar was scared, really scared that it would all come out. And then goodbye career, goodbye Daddy's love, help. He knew, you see. He understood. He knew he had the world if he played it right."

"Didn't he care for Martin at all?"

"Oh, yes, probably. But he's a realist. Nothing for nothing and damn little for a dime. He knew he had to choose. So he did. Guys like him run the world, right?"

"You do go on! Get to cases! So far all I've gotten is a sad fairy story." We grinned at each other.

"Shit. You women are so hard. Don't you have any romance in your soul? Okay, I understand. What happened was old man Borg started smelling a rat. Or something. I'm not sure. Perhaps he got suspicious because the two boys were spending so much time in town in mid-summer. That's not the done thing. They should have been out at the farm swimming or at the Borgs' Georgian Bay cottage. But there was no privacy there so they stayed on in the city. At my place a lot of the time and at the clubs and bars. So old man Borg got curious. Got hold of Oscar and put the pressure on. Oscar chickened out and went home, like a good boy, and Martin just split, like I said. One day he was at my place, the next he was gone. Guitar, packsack and all, That's all I know."

"Got a date on when he left?"

"July, sometime in July. I could check my calendar at home to be more exact."

"Do that. How about Borg? You never met Henry Borg? He never came around to your apartment?"

"Never saw him. If he was there, it must have been while I was out. It's possible, but not likely."

"Why not?"

"Don't be dumb. If he found out that much about me, he would have tried to get me busted or run out of town or something. Guys like him believe they have divine right to make and enforce the rules."

"Not so dumb. He might have been afraid it would all come out about his son. He would have wanted to keep the whole thing quiet. You sure you have not been in touch with him?"

"Now, now. You mean put the black on the rich Mr. Borg? Do I look like a blackmailer?"

"Do blackmailers look any particular way? All right, I believe you. But we still don't know what happened to Martin."

Pause.

Without being asked, Ronnie produced refills for us both. Ottoline never looked up. He was used to perfect service. For a moment we concentrated on our drinks. Then I continued.

"And let's just go over what else you're asking me to believe. That you played indulgent uncle while those two young studs had themselves a honeymoon in your apartment. That you didn't check out their families, who and what they were. That you didn't see the possibilities. And that you had no interest in Martin, personal or professional, and made no move through-out this scene, or try to find out what happened to him after Oscar faded. Nuts! It's not in character, you know it and I know it. So why the hype? Try again."

"No hype. It sure sounds unlikely, but would I make up a story like that? Oh, sure I checked out Millwell and especially old man Borg. That's just common sense. But so what? Do I need that kind of shit? I was sorry to have Martin split. You're right — he *was* special. But it was also a relief. In my business you have to keep your head. So when he left my place I had Ronnie check around to make sure he wasn't hanging out any-where else around. And he wasn't — at least not in the music or gay scenes. So I wrote him off. Figured he went back home. Happens. How's that?"

"Flaky, pretty flaky. Look here, I saw Oscar this morning. He's scared, very nervous. Now it could be that he's scared Daddy will find out about his little escapade. But what's the odds that Daddy knows already? So what's the panic? His frat brothers? The school? All he has to do is deny it. It's gone and past. There's no proof. It's not that big a deal. He could say it's a shakedown. He's over-reacting; as long as Daddy is on his side all else is zilch. So why is he so scared?"

"Oh, you're putting me on. A guy like that can't handle being called a fag. He doesn't accept it, even to himself. Just the possibility that anyone is on to him would freak him out. He doesn't need any other reasons to panic."

"Then what will he do? Tell his father? 'Daddy, please cope ....,' right?"

"Probably. Yes, I'm sure he will. Then you'll have big man Borg himself to deal with. And he's no freshman jock. Watch yourself."

"That's how I figure it too. Thanks. It's nice to have confirmation from an expert. Well, that's all for now. I'll be back. Fill you in on the next thrilling installment. Thanks for your co-operation. I enjoyed this."

"So did I, so did I. Welcome anytime. Drinks on the house, anything. Ronnie!"

"I hear you, Mr Ottoline. Drinks on the house for the lady anytime. Gotcha."

I left.

10

I HAD A FEELING THE NEXT DAY WOULD BE SPECIAL, and it was. Every investigation has at least one moment like that. It was like that when I did legwork in the crummy divorce-and-bad-check business on the Coast. It was like that in U.S. Naval Security sniffing out 'subversives' in the McCarthy fifties. It was like that dealing with dope peddlers, Police finks, cops on the make, in the street scene. And it's like that with respectable people, so-called, in the straight world. You go around asking questions, getting people worried, stirred up. Inevitably, one or more of them starts to act, to do something, to try to confuse the issue, to cover up or to find things out for themselves. It's the normal reaction. Can be counted on. Rather than leave well enough alone, people start making ripples. And all I have to do then is follow them to their source. After my talk with Ottoline I took the night off. Had a pleasant evening. Breakfast in good company the next morning. Sat around at Alex's and waited for developments.

The call came at 11:20 A.M. Mr. Borg's secretary. Would I come and see him that afternoon at his office? Way out in Mississauga. I said I would.

It would be Borg, of course. How did he get my number in Toronto? Easy. After Oscar told him about my visit he called Payne or McPherson. One of them gave him my number and possibly filled him in on who I was and what I was doing. Thus Daddy to the rescue of young son and heir. Nasty, prying female would have to be dealt with. Daddy would do it.

Alex had supplied me with more scoop on Borg. His position as a boot-and-shoe vice-president paid about 45 grand a year, enough to cover running expenses on his three establishments. In no way did it explain how he had acquired them in the first place. House in town. Okay, that was possible. But a cottage in Georgian Bay and hobby farm in Caledon don't come for small change. Inheritance? Stock market? Windfall of some kind? I asked Alex to get me dates and prices on all three of his possessions. Also some idea of how he lived. Did he have other expensive tastes or hobbies like gambling, booze, politics, women, or boys?

McPherson might be a good source for this kind of information. So I called him at the farm.

He was having lunch alone. Katherine was in her studio working, skipping lunch. No wonder she was so thin. He was pleased to hear from me and confirmed unasked that Borg had called him asking about me. That was last night. Young Oscar had gone to the parental home for supper and complained of harrassment. McPherson was amused at the description Borg gave of me.

"Tall, tough dame in *Frye* boots. Very footwear conscious, the Borgs. You scared the darling boy. Tsk, tsk. Borg blamed us, that is me and Katherine, for sicking you on Oscar. Said Martin's disappearance did not justify getting his boy involved. He was very stern with me. I loved it. He's such a jerk!"

"Good. That's all to the good. What else about old Henry? Where does he get his loot and how does he spend it?"

"Where does he get it? What do you mean? Aren't people like him exorbitantly overpaid in business? I always assumed he made a lot, invested, saved, like that. I never made more than $15,000 in my entire life. I have no idea how our capitalist masters do it! But I know he has no expensive vices, except possibly clothes. Dresses well, very manly of course, but expensive. Has a tailor — Steer amd Co., I think. Bay Street somewhere. He travels a good deal on business, but again, I assume all on expense accounts. His wife does have a mink but that's to be expected. She is on the opera committee. Nice lady, well adjusted to her part: she owns the Georgian Bay cottage. Nothing else I can think of about Henry. Drinks of course, but no more than any of his cronies and a hell of a lot less than me." Laughter. "When will you be back to report developments? Katherine would like to know."

I said I would be in touch as soon as I could. Nice and vague, that. I hung up.

Then I pulled on my *Fryes* and left for Mississauga. Toronto no longer has any special rush hours, at least not on the Gardiner Expressway. Maybe it gets a little more congested between 8 and 10 A.M. and again from 4 to 6 P.M., but the difference doesn't amount to a real distinction. At 2 P.M. the road is crowded, full of trucks, delivery vans, and assorted passenger vehicles all trying to beat each other for some reason. Very unlike West Coast Canadians who often drive as if they don't care if they ever get there. Maybe they know something Torontonians have yet to learn.

Actually, I like fast, decisive driving. So I enjoyed the ride. The day was fine, there were sailboats in the lake, Toronto Island looked inviting. I promised myself to visit it before I left.

Universal Shoe Company (Canada) Limited is located on the northern fringes of Mississauga. Landscaped grounds front the three-story office building that hides the low factory at the back. I arrived at the parking lot as a middle-aged man in trim work clothes rode a noisy mower, giving the lawn its last trim of the season. I pulled into a vacant slot marked "Visitors Only", checked the time (it was just on 2:30 P.M.), and walked slowly past the ground-floor office windows to the front door. Inside, I was directed by a security man to what was obviously executive territory — the second-floor mezzanine. A rather formal secretary in 'career girl' clothes and carefully applied makeup asked me to wait. Mr. Borg would see me momentarily. I sat down and checked the reading matter provided for visitors. *Marketing*, *Business Week*, *Shoe and Leather Journal*, and a two-day-old *Globe and Mail*. The whole scene was just too too perfect, like a set for a modern big-business movie designed by someone with no imagination. It was interesting to speculate how someone who worked in such surroundings, someone who was patently, if only partially responsible for them, dealt with unpleasant reality. At a guess he would start by ignoring it, then when that proved impossible would try to make it conform to some pattern which he could accept and handle. He would manipulate matters so that they appeared to fit his preconception. How would he deal with unpleasant reality when this method didn't work? Was Borg capable of action for which he was not programmed? I left the question unanswered, preferring to see him with as open a mind on this issue as was possible in the circumstances.

So far he was acting true to type: he made me wait precisely 20 minutes, not too long but just long enough. When I was finally ushered into his office he started out by being professionally pleasant.

"Good afternoon, Mrs. Keremos. Sorry to keep you waiting. Something always comes up at the most inopportune time. My apologies."

He was a solidly built man in his late forties, tanned, spruce, smiling. His three-piece suit was well cut in the conservative Bay Street fashion. I could not see his shoes, but no doubt they were expensive and well polished. He fitted the decor and everything I had heard about him much too well. Obviously he had a scenario all prepared. If I played my part according to his script he could not lose. A jarring note was called for.

"I'm not married," I said, and went on before he had a chance to apologize again. "You have some information about Martin Millwell's disappearance."

I did not make it a question but a statement. He was momentarily taken aback, as I had intended.

"Information? No! No! What makes you think that?"

"You called and asked to see me. What other reason could you have had? If you don't have any information then there is nothing to discuss."

"My dear Miss Keremos. I did not expect such a forthright young lady. Naturally Oscar, my wife, and I are concerned about Martin. A friend of the family and all that. But we know nothing, nothing about where he has gotten to. How could we? Most likely some scrape or other made him leave town without leaving word. Don't you think that is most likely?"

"No I don't. But what sort of scrape did you have in mind?"

"Well, you know, boys will be boys. Perhaps a girl or some trouble with the law. I believe he got into some fast company when he was here. I don't really know but ...."

"And you asked me out here to tell me that, that you don't know? What fast company, what scrape? Your son spent a lot of time with Martin, right?"

"All right. I see I will have to lay it on the line. It's not pleasant for me in the circumstances since we are friends of the family. But I must insist that you do not bring my son into it. Whatever Martin was up to it had nothing to do with Oscar. I must insist. I have spoken to Don and will speak to Katherine. I will insist that you be given proper instructions on this matter. They hired you, they can stop you from bothering Oscar."

"It won't work. Let's go over this again. Millwell hired me. Katherine Payne fully approves of what I am doing. They are most unlikely to call me off on your say-so. Oscar is scared, would not talk to me, and now you're trying to warn me off. It looks bad. Face it."

"Nonsense! My son knows nothing whatever about Martin. He is busy, his first semester at university. I don't want him bothered and upset. To tell you the truth we had trouble getting him accepted. He is not an outstanding student. So you see it's merely that I don't want him distracted from his studies. He has enough to cope with. That's all. I must insist that you stay away from him."

"It can't be done. He's the obvious source of information. On the contrary, I would suggest that you persuade him to talk to me. It would be better if he told me all he knew. I'll find out what happened this summer anyway. There are other leads, you know. For instance, Ottoline." That really shook him.

"Ottoline! Look here, that man is a gangster! How can you believe one word he says?"

"I don't, necessarily. I don't necessarily believe anyone. And you are being inconsistent, aren't you? On one hand you know nothing, on the other the name Ottoline freaks you out. Borg, we aren't playing games. What your son had to hide may not be relevant to Martin's disappearance. But I must know and I will find out. Much better from him than from someone else. Doesn't that make sense?"

"Look here. This is outrageous. What does Millwell pay you? I'll double it. Leave it alone. Martin will show up when he's ready. Meantime, all you are doing is disturbing innocent people. Just resign this case, go back to Vancouver. I'll make it worth your while. How about it?"

"How much?"

"Ah, now you're talking. Two-thousand dollars?"

"I can be bought, but not cheap, certainly not that cheap. Twenty thousand?"

"Twenty-thousand dollars! Well now, how about $5,000?"

"Forget it."

"Ten, $10,000 and not a penny more!"

"Interesting. So it's worth $10,000 to you for me to drop this case. Why? Don't tell me Oscar's first semester at school is worth that much! You could buy the exam questions for one-hundredth of that. Nuts. You should stick to selling shoes; buying off detectives takes skill. I intend to see Oscar, he *will* talk. Will you help — yes or no?"

"No. I am going to see my lawyer. There must be ways to stop people like you from bothering us. No!"

"Goodbye then Mr. Borg. With or without your help I will find out what happened to Martin Millwell. You may yet wish you were more cooperative."

"Don't you threaten me! Don't you dare! Women like you should not be allowed loose among decent people. Stay away from Oscar, I warn you."

"I'm warned. You are being stupid. Think."

By now I was at the door, leaving a thoroughly shaken and virtually incoherent Henry Borg pounding his desk. Our voices had obviously carried into the outer office. Borg's secretary looked concerned and even a little frightened. I said goodbye politely to her and walked deliberately down the long staircase rather than taking the elevator. The security guard at the desk did not look up.

The incident gave me much to think about. It was apparent that Borg did in fact run true to form. How would he now deal with someone whom he could not con, bully, patronize, bribe, or threaten? And what exactly was he attenptimg to hide — merely Oscar's sexual involvement with Martin, or was there more to it? Oscar's reputation alone could be worth more than $10,000 to Henry, but what a stupid way to play it if that was all he was worried about! After all, chances were that no one except me and Martin's immediate family need know, assuming it was not relevant to Martin's disappearance. I had the problem of figuring out whether Henry was dumb enough to have roused my suspicions like that for what could turn out to be a side issue. It would be in character for him to over-react at the mere idea of homosexuality. But that also had other implications.

11

THIS WAS A SITUATION OF DO-NOT-STOP, do-not-leave-them-time-to-think. I went directly to Oscar's frat on Huron Street. This time of day it presented a somewhat different appearance. The big TV was tuned to a soap opera. A few be-denimed bodies distributed around it in the large front room paid no attention to anything. All but one were male. The exception was a young woman, a woman I remembered from McPherson's class at the FArt. Coincidence? She was sitting reading, obviously waiting for someone or something. She looked up expectantly as I entered. Surprise!

"If this is coincidence, it has a mightly long arm," I said, quite friendly. She was disconcerted, as well she might be.

"No, I guess it's not. A coincidence, I mean." She stopped, searching for words.

"Let me guess. Don McPherson sent you here to see Oscar. Right?"

"But, how did you know? Yes, he asked me to find out .... things. We didn't expect you here. I can't say any more. Please, please go away. She was not good at dealing with the spot she had gotten into. I cursed McPherson for using her for whatever it was he was up to. Didn't have the nerve to handle it personally so he was getting her involved; a student who was obviously more than slightly in love with him. Of course she might be part of the puzzle, but I doubted it. But Don sure as hell wasn't just part of the scenery. Otherwise why? I intended to find out, but meanwhile she had to be helped out of this situation.

"Look .... what's your name?"

"Gale. Gale Mangoni. I was just doing Don a favor, he's worried, you know. He worries a lot. I was just trying to help. I don't even know Oscar."

"Go home. Leave it to me. I'll talk with Don and explain. There's nothing you can do. You did your best. It's okay."

She was relieved to leave, smart enough to know she was out of her depth.

"And don't do any more favors like that for Don or any other prick who asks you. Don't spend your life looking after their interests; look after your own."

I don't ordinarily give advice, but I was too mad to care. I knew I was not playing it smart; I should have gotten her to tell me what Don wanted from Oscar. But all I wanted was to get her out of there.

I watched her run down the front steps and then went looking for Oscar's room. It turned out to be on the second floor. The door was not locked. I went in and started going through it methodically. It was unlikely that I would find anything since he had moved in only a few weeks earlier, long after Martin had vanished. But you never know, there might be something illuminating, and anyway it would help me to figure out Oscar. And it did, in a negative sort of way. The room was safe. There was nothing to suggest anything but the most conventional interests. Like his father he was oh so typical. A freshman jock in engineering. A squash racket, three pairs of running shoes, the traditional pinups, sports magazines, an unopened package of safes, lots of dirty laundry, a few porno paperbacks available in any cigar store, newspaper clippings of sports events, picture of a woman who was probably his mother. The usual junk. No personal correspondence. All I found for my trouble was a card for a place for gay males called The Barracks, used as a bookmark in a reference book on mechanics. It could have been left there by anyone. I sat down to wait for Oscar knowing full well that he might not be back for hours, perhaps not at all that day. But it was worth the chance that he would come back to change his clothes before going home to see his father again. My hunch worked. At 5:40 he walked in. And almost walked out again when he saw me.

"Don't tell me you had any illusion that you had seen the last of me? Sit down, man, and talk to me. And this time I mean talk. I don't feel very patient towards the Borgs today. Your sainted Daddy pissed me off. So no more vanishing acts. You stay here and talk."

"You saw Dad and didn't he .... What happened? What did he say?"

"He didn't scare or buy me off if that's what you want to know. Aren't you a little too big to be running home to him? It won't help anyway. I saw Ottoline yesterday, dig? No more secrets. So spit it all out like a good boy."

Oscar seemed to go into shock. His lips twitched. He sat down heavily on the bed and put his head in his hands. We were going to get a little puerile dramatics.

"Stop the great tragedy number. Just tell me what happened before I start bouncing you off the walls."

"I can't, really. I can't. It's all so painful, so horrible," he bawled.

"Nuts. You had a hot affair with Martin. So what? No big deal. Where is Martin? What happened to him? I'm not leaving here until you open up so you may as well decide to come out with it."

"It was all Nate's fault. He made us do it. You don't understand. He .... turned us on to each other. We didn't know what we were doing. We're under age .... under 21 .... it's all his doing. Why don't you get after him?"

"Save all that shit for Daddy. Who do you think you're trying to snow with that jive? I don't give a damn about your love life. I want to know what happened to Martin. Get that through your head, you schmuck. All the bullshit in the world won't prevent me from getting the truth out of you! So smarten up. Talk."

Suddenly he was on his feet and making for the door. There was nothing for it. I hit him in the stomach hard, and as he doubled up hit him again backhanded across the side of the head. It was like hitting a child except that he was a 6'2" ball player and outweighed me by 50 lbs. There's no time for niceties in such circumstances. He fell like a ton of dirty laundry and lay doubled up in a fetal position. I grabbed his ears, pulled him up to half-sitting, and proceeded to slap his face alternately with both hands.

"Now you will talk, you little fart. You will talk, believe me, or this is nothing to what I will do to you. And Daddy is not here to protect you. Get hold or yourself and answer my questions."

"Stop it, stop it! I'll tell you all I know but I don't know what happened to Martin. Honest, I don't"

His face was red with white marks from my hands.

"So tell me."

I stepped back and leaned against the door frome looking down at this poor excuse for a human being. I have no trouble restraining my sympathy for the rich and fortunate. The sight of Oscar made me slightly sick and very mad. Mostly I resented being made to treat Oscar this way, the most efficient way to get what I wanted. It reinforced all that his father had made him. He was used to being bullied; the beating was nothing. He would tell me what he knew because he was used to obeying. And he would continue to be bullied and manipulated all his life by anyone stronger than himself. At best he would be sly, nasty, and a liar, in self-defense. And in turn take it out on others whenever he might have any advantage. Weak, helpless people often do. But towards the powerful he was subservient, without courage. Henry Borg had a lot to answer for. Oscar still sat on the floor, holding his gut and sobbing. I made an impatient move and he started.

"I was spending all this time in town with Martin. Nate told you, so you know. I would go home for dinner once in a while. To see my mother, mostly. Then one might Dad just told me I was not to go back, ever. He .... he made quite a scene. Made me see what I was doing to myself. Made me see .... So I went to the cottage with Mother the next day. And Dad said he would talk to Martin, explain that it was all over. And I never saw him again. I wanted to but I never did. That's all, that's all I know. You've got to believe me!"

"Not so fast. Didn't your father ever mention what happened

between him and Martin? When did they meet and where?"
I was pretty gentle.

"Oh yes. I can tell you that. Well, Mother and I got to the
cottage — it's near Honey Harbour — on Saturday, by noon.
Then Dad arrived next day, that would be Sunday, in mid-July,
I don't remember the date but the Olympics were on. He arrived
and told me that he had called Martin; I gave him the phone
number of Nate's apartment you see, and Martin had come up
to the farm the night before. Then, well .... oh! I hate this ....
Dad had bought him off! Really, really Martin sold out for
$5,000! I saw the receipt, I did. What could I do?" He was cry-
ing real tears.

"Steady on. So on Friday you came home for dinner and were
told not to see Martin again. On Saturday you and your mother
left Toronto for the cottage. Your father stayed in town, so why
did Martin meet him at the farm?"

"Well, Dad had some business there, I think there was an
auction in the afternoon he wanted to attend. So he arranged
for Martin to come up Saturday night. It's not far. And that's
when he paid him to go away and not see me again. Not to
write even. Just to disappear. Martin always wanted to travel,
you know. Down to the States, Mexico, South America. So Dad
just made it easy for him. I couldn't believe it, I couldn't. But
I saw the receipt and then when there was no word from Martin,
well, I had to accept it, didn't I?"

It was pathetic; he wanted so much for me to believe him.

"So on Sunday your father arrived and told you he had gotten rid of Martin. And showed you a receipt for $5,000. How
did he pay him? In cash?"

"He said he paid cash. That's all he said."

"How did he have $5,000 in cash on a Saturday? And what
did the receipt say exactly?"

"I don't know, he just did. And the receipt was just a receipt
for $5,000 signed by Martin. I know his signature. It was his,
and anyway, why would Dad lie? The truth was bad enough."

"Maybe. What happened then?"

"Well, Dad arrived and I think he stayed till Tuesday, but Mother and I went to Montreal on Monday for the last week of the Olympics. It had all been arranged long before. Then when I got back .... Martin was long gone."

"And you never inquired after him? His mother lives next door to your farm. You weren't interested in where he went, whether she had heard from him?"

"Dad told me not to. He said to leave it alone. Just forget Martin, the whole thing. Then it was September, I had to go to school, my first semester, you know. I got busy. Anyway, I didn't want to know; I wanted to forget. It hurt too much."

He was crying again. Letting it come out, feeling the pain. I decided I had gotten enough, at least for now.

"Okay, if you told me the truth. You better have. If I find you lied ...."

"No, no, it's the truth. Honest!" Little boy and his Scout's honor.

"Now let me give you a word of advice." It was my day for good advice to the innocent young. "Clean yourself up. Go to a movie, go to the baths, go dancing. Don't call your father, don't go home, Don't let him find you for at least 24 hours. Got me?"

"Okay, okay. But why? He'll be mad. And Mother will worry."

"Your father will be mad at you anyway when he finds out that you talked to me. And what about Martin's mother? Who cares that she worries! Just do what I say. Your father is mad at me already. You can say I beat you and tied you up. You want to do that?"

"No, I guess not. I'll just say you upset me so I got drunk. I probably will, anyway."

"I don't care what you do, just be hard to find for a day or so. I'm going to find out exactly what happened from your father and I don't want you underfoot. Understood?"

"All right. I'll do what you say. I guess I have no choice. I never had any, really."

"That's right — no choice."

No choice! This beautiful rich young white male creature had no choice! He could rationalize it any way he liked. It was none of my business.

I left Oscar still sitting on the floor. It was a little after six o'clock.

12

THERE WERE A FEW MINOR CHORES TO BE DONE. I got Alex onto the passport office in Ottawa and the Mexican consulate. Not that I expected anything from it but it's a good idea to be thorough. Then I called Katherine Payne and announced I was coming out to see her. No word to or about McPherson. Let him stew. She told me Millwell had been trying to reach me all day for a progress report. I said I would handle that. She asked me if I had any news; I said "so long".

Next I called Borg's farm. A woman answered and said that Mr. and Mrs. Borg were not there but that Mr. Borg was expected the next day. I hung up. Then I went to a good cheap Chinese place on Spadina, had a beautiful dinner, then a few beers with the folks at the Paramount Tavern.

By nine I was on the road again. Like the day, the night was clear but cool. I drove past the McPherson mailbox to the next drive. This mailbox said *Henry Borg, Esq.*, and the drive was barred by a solid, white painted gate. I opened it and drove through. The Borg property was not your usual Ontario farm. It had all the marks of a gentleman's country estate: citified house with pillars, long lines of white fences, black wrought-iron carriage lamps throwing yellow light onto the well-kept lawn and outbuildings. There was a stable complete with horses, a barn with a shiny new roof, and what looked like a manager's cottage tucked away behind the stables. A thick hedge hid the swimming pool. I drove to what I took to be the manager's cottage. Lights were on and as I pulled up the door opened. A youngish man in cowboy boots stood and waited for me to approach him.

"Evening. I heard in Caledon that Borg was looking for help around the horses. I just arrived from B.C. looking for work."

With my jeans, boots, heavy tan, and rough, dark hair, I do look the part — sort of. And 'horsey' people do travel around from stable to stable.

"Mr. Borg is not here. He does the hiring. I don't think we need anyone, but you might want to come back tomorrow. He never tells me his plans."

I stood there trying to look tired and interesting at the same time. He bit.

"Well, come in. Have a cup of coffee and tell me what kind of work you've done. You may as well rest up a bit. Molly .... company," he shouted to someone inside the house.

That's how I spent most of an hour, pumping Jerry and Molly Sharpe, the couple who looked after Borg's farm. Molly was English. She had been a school teacher and liked to impart information, which she did in a high nasal whine. Jerry was quintessentially a small-town, Anglo-Canadian; a flat voice, broad a's and expressions like "yea big" and "irregardless". Both were very, very talkative. A nice enough couple, unsuspecting and straightforward, interested in their employers. With very little prompting I learned about the Borgs, their comings and goings, their six horses and 80-odd head of cattle, the summer parties at the pool, their money, cars, and friends. The Sharpes had been there over a year. He had been with the Armed Forces in Germany where he and Molly met. She was visiting from England. They married, and on his discharge had come to Toronto where he got a job as a security guard at Universal Shoe. Borg apparently hand-picked the security people personally and when he learned that Jerry knew about horses, had offered them both this job. The previous manager, inherited with the property, had quit.

"It's a big job for two people. How do you manage?"

"Well, we don't have much to do with the cattle. Mr. Borg buys them to fatten up on grass, then sells them. A local farmer looks after all that. We look after the house, clean, and help Mrs. Borg if there's a party. But they aren't here a lot and sometimes we don't even se them when they are here. But the horses and grounds .... boy, that's a lot of work. We get local help once in a while. It could be that Borg is thinking of hiring someone like you. Do you want to live in? There's a room next to the tack room you could have, I guess."

"It would be okay if Borg was not around all the time. I like horses, but rich owners are a pain."

"Oh, in summer they're around, especially young Oscar. Always in the pool. But they have a cottage and they travel. Don't really know why Borg bought this place. I guess when he came into all that money from his father he wanted a country place. It's the fashionable thing around here. He's interested in keeping it up first class and spends a lot of money on it. But he isn't up here all that often. Boy, it would be nice to be rich like that."

"More trouble than it's worth, in my opinion. Always driving back and forth, moving furniture and bits and pieces from one house to the other."

"That's true. Boy, this summer they were in and out of here; back to Toronto, on to the cottage. Half the time nobody knew where anybody was, when they would arrive, or where the cars were. Sometimes it's a real comedy routine just discussing who will take which car where and when."

There followed an animated discussion of the lifestyles and vagaries of the rich, so often interesting to the less affluent. It was not getting me anywhere so I forced a change of topic. This can be a dangerous tactic, as it immediately becomes clear that the conversation is being managed.

"Do you visit much around here? What are the neighbors like?"

I was pumping outrageously, but they were so starved for company they were not about to turn me off.

"Well, there are still real farmers in these parts but fewer and fewer. Now, right next door, you must have passed their drive, there are a couple of artists. Very nice people, but keep to themselves. Don McPherson, he and Mr. Borg know each other from way back. Not that they are close; in fact, they fight every time they meet. But Katherine's boy, Martin, is a friend of Oscar's. Funny, Martin was here once this summer when Oscar was away at the cottage, remember that Molly?"

"Yes, that was the day Mr. Borg bought Jenny, the new filly, at the auction. Seven-hundred dollars he paid. Outrageous. That Martin boy must have hitchhiked in and out, never saw any strange cars or saw him come and go. But the two of them certainly had a set-to that evening."

"Right, that's when it was. We went out that night — it was Saturday — for a few beers in town. So we never saw him leave. Oh, well. Still, I sometimes wonder what that was all about. Why did Martin come here with Oscar away? Never happened before that I recall. Mr. Borg never has a civil word about any of them next door."

"Maybe he just came over for a swim." I laughed. "Or do they have a pool next door?"

"No, they don't. It's not a fancy place at all. But you should see the pool here — really great! No expense spared. It's some pool! So maybe that's what happened: Martin wanted a swim. Never know about these kids. Just do whatever they want when they want to. Yeah, I guess that could explain it."

"Who cares anyway? Spoilt bunch, the lot of them."

And we were back on the oddities of their employers. It was getting late and I didn't want to outstay my welcome. So I finished my third cup of coffee and thanked Molly and Jerry for their hospitality.

"Time I was going back. I'll call Mr. Borg tomorrow, see if he wants a stable hand. Maybe I'll just check in next door and see if they have any work. See you again. And thanks."

"Welcome. Drive careful now. Bye."

13

IT WAS AFTER ELEVEN WHEN I PULLED IN at the Payne-McPherson property. Lights were on in the kitchen and the studio. I went in the back door, which opened directly into the kitchen. McPherson sat at the table surrounded by empty beer bottles. He looked up, his eyes bleary. My face must have communicated something to him for he stood up suddenly and started to babble aggressively.

"You're late, damn you! What do you mean coming here at this hour, keeping us waiting? You hired keyhole peeper .... What are you up to?"

"Cut it, McPherson. What are *you* up to .... sending Gale to spy on Oscar? Can't you at least do your own dirty work? And you lied to me about Borg's money. You knew he inherited from his father. What's all this to you? I bet I know. I bet you think you can get to Borg somehow through Oscar. A shakedown, maybe? Lies, little sneaky prying and an opportunity to squeeze some bread from your old enemy. You always envied Borg, didn't you? All that self-righteous liberal bullshit about 'our capitalist masters'. You would love to be in Henry's shoes. You nasty little phony. Didn't have a chance to get in on the gravy train like Borg and so now you're all bitterness and sour grapes. You make me sick. If I thought you actually had anything to do with Martin's disappearance, I would have your neck. But you don't have the guts to take any real action, good or bad. You just feed on fallout from other people's lives."

I would have gone on for a while, with him standing there with his mouth open, but at that point Katherine walked into the room. She had obviously heard — enough.

"That's enough. Don, please leave us. I want to talk to Helen. Now!"

Her voice was strained but firm. Don left without a word, only a dirty look at me.

"Now what's all this about? You shouldn't bully Don. He can't take it."

"You knew about Don and now I know about Don. And you both knew about Martin and Oscar, about their relationship. You knew your son was gay. Why not tell me? And you must have known that Don would try to use this knowledge somehow. What sort of games are you playing?"

"No games, the last thing I want is to play any games. I just want everything to settle down with a minimum of pain and fuss. Don would never have managed to blackmail Borg. He hasn't got it in him to be a villain. It wouldn't have done any good to interfere. His ego is sensitive as it is. Borg can look after himself. I shed no tears for Borg."

"No tears for Borg, right. But don't you realize that Don could have been in danger, real danger? Borg is no patsie. You really haven't been thinking. Well, it's time to start."

"I don't understand. Tell me."

She had gone very still, the way I had seen her on my last visit. We sat down at opposite sides of the kitchen table.

"All right. Listen. Some of this is still supposition but I bet my license on it. Here is the scenario in shorthand. Martin and Oscar were having a love-affair this summer in Toronto. Staying at Uncle Nate's — that's Ottoline, of course. You must have guessed that much."

"Yes."

"Borg found out, decided to stop it — and did. That's all."

"What do you mean 'that's all'? How did he stop it?"

"I believe that Borg killed your son."

Silence. She did not move, hardly blinked. A long sigh.

"That's what I feared all along. Martin disappeared without a word. It was so unlike him. He was such a fine, fine man, a good son, sensitive person. Oh, why ...."

"Katherine. Don't. Don't let yourself go, not yet. There will be time for grief, for pain. Lots of time. Now please help me. There are decisions to make, steps I have to take. First of all, is there anything you've been keeping from me? Any details about Martin or Borg or anything that happened this summer?"

"No, I don't think I know anything useful. Martin had told me about Oscar. He said he was in love, wanted me to understand and approve. I did the mother bit, I said anything that made him happy .... I saw no great problem. People should be allowed to live their lives. I guess I was not really aware of how the world views these things, and creatures like Borg are quite outside my comprehension. I mean I knew he would not like it but I had no idea to what lengths he would go. What do we do now?"

"Just a minute. You told Don. Why didn't you tell Millwell?"

"There was no need, really. Millwell knew. I suspect he knew all along about Martin. That's why he hired you, you see that?"

"Yes, I figured that out. A woman like me would be able to handle it better than a male private investigator, who would probably be an ex-cop. And I was not local; there was less chance it would get out where it could hurt anyone. I see that."

"Right. The moment I saw you I knew James knew. He's quite bright, you know. And both upright and uptight. He would see it as his duty to have Martin's disappearance properly investigated, but he would arrange it carefully to do him — and me, I guess — the least harm. He has a reputation to protect."

"Will he protect Borg, then? If, as I suspect, Borg killed your son, will he be willing to have it all come out?"

"Probably. He has a sense of justice. Rather abstract sense, but strong."

"Okay. I'll report to him exactly what I think happened. But so far I have no proof, no proof at all against Borg. Even the circumstantial evidence is hazy. I'll have to blow Borg's cover and that won't be easy. Do I have your support?"

"Of course. Do what you must. I'll talk to James on my own. I'm sure he will approve. Do you need more money? I'll write you a check right now. Then both of us will be your clients."

"Yes. I could use another five-hundred. Millwell's retainer is long gone. And this next stage could be tricky and take some time. Are you sure you want me to go on? It could get messy."

"My god, Martin was my son! What do you take me for? I must know exactly what happened, where his body is .... Do you know?"

I did not remind her that she had not been so positive about it before.

"I can guess, but let's leave it at that. Okay. That's clear then. Now what about friend Don? What do you propose we do about him and his little scheme? You realize he's been trying to blackmail Borg. I suspect just about Oscar's sexual preference, not about murder. He wouldn't risk shaking down a murderer who had nothing to lose by making it a double-header. Nice fellow, Don. How come you're still together? You know what he is."

"Oh, I know. But I want him, you see. He suits me. Let's face it, we suit each other. It's what is called a symbiotic relationship. I don't much like myself for it but he suits me. So leave him alone. I'll handle him. Just as long as Borg doesn't take steps to get him. I want Don protected."

"I can't protect Don directly but I can promise you Borg will be too busy trying to get rid of me to bother with Don — so long as Don keeps out of it as of right now. Can you be sure he will? He's greedy and wants money badly."

"Yes." That's all she said, just yes. I had to accept it.

"Okay. Now let's call Millwell in Winnipeg. I'll brief him and then you can talk to him as you wish. And that check: that would be useful."

"Let me get my checkbook."

She went out of the kitchen and was back with a check a few minutes later.

"Let's use my private line in the studio. There are no extensions." She knew McPherson.

We talked to Millwell for a good half-hour. His voice on the line was careful and tense. The strain was showing. He and Katherine trusted each other, even though there was no love or even much liking. Two very, very different people both trying to do the right thing, both loving their son. I made my report and they both agreed to leave the next steps to me.

I didn't leave until close to 2 A.M. It had been a long day. I was tired and depressed. McPherson had not reappeared.

14

NEXT DAY WAS COOL AND BRIGHT just like the previous one. It was hard to believe only 24 hours had passed since I had received the invitation to visit Borg at his office. From now on I would have to be more calculating: each step had to be thought out. Not that it would work exactly the way it was planned but just to avoid major errors. It might be important to get to Borg before he got to his son. I wondered whether Oscar had obeyed my instructions and made himself scarce. A call to his frat confirmed that he was out and had been out all night. Good. Chances were that Borg had not been able to find him either. I called Borg and was put through immediately.

"I want to see you," I said, no preliminaries.

"Oh, you do, do you! Why should I see you?"

"I know what happened to Martin. You might be interested in hearing about it."

"Interested? Well, I guess I can manage to see you for a few minutes this afternoon."

"In an hour — and not in your office!"

"What! Don't give me orders. Forget it."

"I saw Oscar again yesterday. He talked."

"What happened? Where is he?"

"I'll see you in High Park at twelve exactly. I will be parked at the restaurant near Grenadier Pond in a green camper pickup with B.C. plates. You'll find me."

"Okay, okay, I'll be there. It had better be good."

"It will be."

My next call was to Ottoline. I couldn't reach him so I left a message that I wanted to see him that evening. Ronnie was very obliging. On the way to High Park I bought myself a hot Italian veal sandwich on a Kaiser and a pint of milk. I burped hot peppers for 20 minutes but felt better all the same.

It's hard to describe the encounter with Borg. He was by turns threatening and pathetic, cool and aggressive, loud and charming, mildly annoyed and terribly frightened. But he never entirely lost control of himself. Even when confronted by his own lies and pushed to account for them, he admitted nothing. He still believed the situation could be retrieved.

His story, as I described it to Ottoline that evening, was simple.

"See Nate, Borg's not used to losing. This turkey does not believe it can happen to him. Guess it never has. So first of all, Oscar is not a homosexual. Henry can't admit it, he can't face that. So it has to be that you and Martin were in a plot to ruin his son. And all he did was save him from 'the gay menace'. He actually said that any action on his part would be justified under the circumstances and any decent person would accept and support that stand. Absolutely anything goes."

"So he did admit he had done something."

"Yes, but nothing like murder. No, he sticks to his bribery story just as Oscar described it. But he defends himself as if to a murder charge before a jury of his peers. It could be in fact that he senses his peers would understand his rationale for murder. He doesn't believe it needs to come to that, a murder trial, but he has his arguments all ready."

"You mean justifiable homicide? He could be right, you know. It's okay to ice fags, isn't it?"

"Something like that. His argument is that once all else fails, like persuasion, threats or bribery, killing is the only way out. But he also claims that bribery did not fail, that Martin took his five thousand and split. That would prove Martin never cared for Oscar in the first place, and that in turn would prove that Henry was right about it all being a nasty plot."

"What's my part supposed to be in this scenario?"

"Well, that's the interesting part. He says that if Martin did get iced, then you did it. Of course he can't know for sure, but the scenario is that Martin came back to town, and you killed him to get your hands on the five thousand cash. What do you think of that?"

"Bull .... What do you think?"

"Bull or not, there are some unexplained things. Like Martin's gear. What happened to it? You said one day it was at your place, next it was gone, along with Martin. Now, Martin did go to Borg's farm that Saturday, but Henry claims he did not have his pack and guitar with him. Why should he?"

We were sitting at a corner table upstairs at Nate's favorite eatery. Onion soup, *escargots*, good white wine. A pleasant young man was singing softly, competing with the low early Friday-night hubbub.

"Henry's pretty cute. As he points out there is no body so it's all academic and we can go piss up a rope as far as accusations are concerned. And he's right. You realize that he was smart enough to stick exactly to the story he told Oscar, even though he did not know what Oscar had told me? He had not been able to check that, you see. And that was the safest tack to take, no doubt of it."

"What's all this leading up to? Are you saying you're stumped or you believe him or what? And how about all that jive about Martin's gear and the five thousand that I was supposed to off him for. You follow that up?"

"Well, sure. It's got to be checked out. And no, I'm not stumped. But it will take some fancy footwork from now on."

"Seems to me your footwork has been pretty fancy all along, including right now. You want something from me; are you trying to maneuver me into something? That's what it feels like at my end. And I don't like it."

"Nate, for a smart dude you're slow. Naturally I'll have to clear up some loose ends — like what happened to Martin's gear. He could have taken it with him, meaning to join Oscar, or perhaps go back home to Winnipeg or like that. Or someone could have snuck it out of your pad. It's all possible. But without a body it's all smoke. Right?"

"Right. So?"

"So use your head."

"This is your gig, you tell me."

"You want a diagram, okay. Let's assume that Henry iced Martin and disposed of the body. Only he knows where. And it's probable that there is something about the body or where it's hidden that points right at him as the killer. Like if he buried it in his backyard or dumped it in Georgian Bay near his cottage. That would make it very awkward for him if it was found. Follow me so far?"

"Don't get so smart. Go on."

"So how do we find Martin's body? There are two ways to look for it. One is dig up half the country, drag the lake. No way without the cops and they would laugh me out of town with what I got up to now. So that way is out. It's just not practical. There's only one other way."

"Sure. Get Henry to show you. Fat chance."

"But a chance, our only chance. Now why would he do that? How can we force his hand? There's only one motive as far as I can see for Henry to produce the body or allow it to be found."

"I'll bite."

"You're a great straight man, you know that? It's simple. There must be a better candidate for the killer role. Someone else he can pin the murder on. So what I'm saying is, if we crowd him but at the same time have another good suspect he might decide that Martin's disappearance must be solved. And it won't be until Martin or his body reappears. Follow?"

"Hey, I follow, and I like it even less. You have me picked out as the 'better candidate'. It smells like a frame. Forget it."

"I didn't pick you, that would be no good. No, Henry the turkey is already leading me there. All we have to do is go along until he feels safe in producing the *corpus delicti*."

"*We*, what *we*? You kidding? Want me to cooperate in my own frame? You are nuts."

"What's the alternative?"

"Well, 20 years in Kingston for Nate Ottoline ain't no alternative, that's for sure. So you dig up the body and then Henry hangs it on me? And with your help? That may be a solution for you, but it sure ain't for me."

"Get real. Nobody said anything about hanging it on you. Just make it look like a way out to Henry. Once it's established that Martin died, and how he died, that's all we need."

"Because under our perfect system of justice the innocent are never falsely convicted and the guilty never go unpunished? What are you trying to sell me? This is not a grade-five social studies textbook. It's real. And between Henry Borg, solid citizen, and Nate Ottoline, who will the cops believe? And who'll they try to railroad into Kingston?"

"Have faith, brother, faith. It will never come to that, I promise. No cops!"

"Promise! A lot of good your promises will do! You think Henry couldn't rig it up so it points right at me. He's trying to do that now, before there is any real murder investigation. And I thought you were smart! Shit, just don't you try any of your tricks at my expense. I warn you."

"Like I said, there's no alternative. I even thought of Don McPherson for the part but he doesn't fit as well. It's you or nothing."

"Then it's nothing. You know, your nerve amazes me. Never saw such chutzpa. Why should I care whether you solve this case or not? Forget it and go home if you can think of nothing better than to involve me!"

"You are already involved — and I have no intention of dropping it. Like you said, it's my scene and I know what I am doing. I don't really think you have a choice. I'm just telling you this as a matter of courtesy, I'm not asking."

"I hear you. And it sounds like a threat. How do you propose to carry this through without putting my neck in a noose?"

"Thought you would never ask."

"Now I'm asking. So tell me."

So I told him. He listened silently, a sceptical look on his face.

"And what if you're wrong? What if it doesn't work out this way?"

"Well, I could be wrong. Maybe Henry didn't do it, that's one possibility. Maybe he's shielding Oscar or just trying to make life difficult for me. Want to give me odds on that?"

"No way. I buy Henry as the heavy. But he may not play; he could get cagey. What then?"

"Then I'm back where I started. If he doesn't lead me to Martin's body you're safe and we're no worse off. Would have to try something else. Stay flexible on that score. But it can work. And all the risk is mine, not yours. So what's to sweat?"

"It's risky all right. Would take a lot of nerve. Why would you take a risk like that? What's in it for you?"

"Call it dumb. Call it what you like. That's how I play my hands. To the end."

"Well, it's your life. Remind me not to play cards with you, wil you. You play too close to the bone. I like better odds than that."

"Correction. The odds *are* good. It's up to me not to blow it, that's all. Don't you think I can pull it off?"

"As between you and Henry, my money's on you. But there are so many unknowns. Hell, anything could happen!"

"Not quite 'anything'."

"Yeah, I know. Your mind's made up. And you love the suspense. Me, I prefer Russian roulette."

"Which you wouldn't play either. We each get our jollies as best we know how. Well, enough of that. I'm ready for another cognac. How about you?"

"Make it two. Waiter, make it two more."

15

NEXT TWO DAYS WERE A WEEKEND and nothing much happened. Except two dudes tried to put me away.

I had spent most of Saturday tidying up loose ends, checking things over with Alex, all the bits and pieces. Like, how hard was it to remove something from Nate's apartment and what had the situation been there the weekend of July 24 and 25. And then there was Don McPherson. Now that he had brought himself into the picture I needed a clearer view of his doings.

Among all these things I tried to get to Henry Borg by phone. I finally got him at the farm. I had a simple request: would he show me the farm and then take me up to the cottage. At first he was so furious with me for 'beating up' his son as he called it that I had difficulty making him listen. Suddenly he got very quiet and serious. Why did I want to go to the Georgian Bay cottage? What did I expect to gain by going over the farm?

"Just yes or no," I said. "I want to know exactly what happened when Martin came to see you that Saturday at the farm. What was said and done, where and when. Reconstruct, sort of. That clear? And I also want to see your cottage."

"Why? What's all this .... First you beat up my son .... I could have you arrested for that, and now you're making demands. Why should I ....?"

"Cool it. Listen. You will do it because you have to. This mess is not just going to go away. I want answers and you'll help me this time. Unless it's not in your interest to get at the truth? How about it?"

"Of course I want the truth! But who says it has anything to do with me?"

"Hey, turkey! Get it through your head that your bribery-and-farewell story just doesn't scan. Nobody believes it. Get it? I'm giving you a chance to prove to me that it really happened. So persuade me. I'm doing you a favor."

"All right, all right. Come to the farm Monday morning. Then we'll go up to the cottage. Anything to get this thing out of the way. You're ruining my son ...."

"Spare me the pathos. See you Monday, A.M."

I rang off in his ear. It was all set. And it was Saturday night with nothing to do until Monday. So I looked up a friend and we went out on the town. First to a Jarvis Street bar, then over to a club in the East End. It was after 2 A.M. when I finally found a parking spot a good two blocks from Alex's house. Side streets on the Beaches are very quiet at that time of night. Even the boardwalk is empty of joggers, dogs, and their walkers. Full of booze, I stopped to look at the lake.

It happened very fast. As I turned I became conscious of two figures converging on me from behind the lines of parked cars which line the access road. Anywhere else it could have been taken for a simple attempt at mugging. But it is rare in Toronto and anyway, this was not a good area. Who would be a likely victim. No, these two turkeys were there to get me. All that was clear to me in that split second before the first one got to me. The other was a step behind.

I am not an expert in Kung Fu or Karate. Just plain, simple street fighting. And in that, booze even helps. It makes you reckless and unafraid of pain. And that's what it takes. The first one — he was small and dark — I kicked in the stomach. It's a big target and sensitive. It was not a very good kick but effective enough to slow him down. He mis-stepped, tripped on the curb, and fell. By then the other one — big and white — was on me. His right fist hit my shoulder as he tried to grab me with his left hand. I twisted my body away, drove my elbow into his guts and followed it up by a side chop to the head. By then his pal was up and making for me. I turned and butted his stomach again with my head as he came charging. His own impetus did him in. He fell with a gurgle, out of it. Pain, and probably a broken rib.

The big dude didn't wait fo find out. He took off. But not before I got a good look at him in the street light. I had seen that scared, white face before but right then I couldn't remember where. Never mind, the other one was out of commission and would be persuaded to answer a few questions.

I grabbed his right arm, twisting it behind his back. He moaned. There was blood on his face where he had bitten through his lip. I propped him up against a parked car and examined him. He was black, and from his mumbled speech, West Indian.

"No more, Missis, no more. Let me go. I didn't mean nothing."

"Who hired you?" I went through his pockets; his wallet held no identification except for an employee card in the name of Irving Farmer from Alnight Industrial Cleaners: *We Clean while you Dream*, odds and ends, and some money — five crisp new $10 bills.

"Who hired you? And what were you hired to do? Beat me up? Kill me? For fifty bucks! What? Talk." To encourage him I drove my knee into his crotch. It wasn't necessary.

"Not kill, not kill! Just rough up a bit. That's all. He didn't say you would fight. Just an easy fifty. Easy!" he groaned.

"Who?"

"I don't know, Missis. Ed, he just said, 'Want to make an easy fifty bucks?' I said 'sure'. That's all."

"Who's Ed?"

"He's run away. Big guy like that, runs away."

"What's his full name?"

"Ed Wintermans. He said we put you away in hospital for a week and we get a bonus, that's what he say. That's all I know."

"Where do you work?"

"Nowhere now, Missis, been laid off. Used to work cleaning nights. Now no money coming in, need money bad. Ed, he know that, do me a favor, let me make a few dollar. That's what he say. You gonna let me go now? I told you all I know."

"Irving, you an illegal?"

"No, no, Missis, I'm landed, truly!"

"Well, we'll soon find out at the cop shop. First thing they'll do is check with Immigration. You won't just take a fall for assault, you'll get deported!''

"You wouldn't do that." He might be in a spot but he had me figured out in no time.

"Why not? Why shouldn't I? You're not telling all you know, are you? Tell me something I can believe and I'll let you go. What instructions were you given? Now!''

"Okay, okay. Ed said we beat you up good, put you in hospital. 'Out of action', he said, 'put her out of action.' If we get caught we say nothing .... 'Keep you mouth shut' he said, Ed said, 'or Mr. Ottoline will turn you in to the police for sure.' That's all I know.''

"Mr. Ottoline! So he hired Ed and Ed hired you. Is that what you're saying?"

"That's right, that's all I know. Now let me go, I think I broke something, it hurts." His voice and manner changed; he had dropped his protective 'black face' role, which he used for survival in a white man's country.

"Probably a cracked rib. Yes, you need a doctor. Get a cab on Queen Street, go to Emergency at Wellesley maybe. Here, keep the fifty bucks. Get yourself fixed up and disappear. Don't let Ed find you. Clear?''

"Clear. And thanks."

I watched him walk away holding his side. He'd been set up because he was black and illegal. But then I remembered where I had seen big, white Ed before. Very careless of him to let me see his face.

16

IT MAY SOUND LIKE IT HAD BEEN EASY, but in fact I had bruises in places I didn't even know had been hit. That's what happens in a fight. You don't feel things until later. Alex woke up when I came in and did a ministering angel bit. Rough and ready as she was, it was nice. Once the adrenalin ceased pumping, pain had hit me. Finally, full of brandy and other painkillers, I fell asleep. Next day, after a hot bath and a good meal, I felt okay. I filled Alex in on what had happened and she was properly indignant.

"That bum Ottoline! Are you going to stand for this? Let's get him! Let's go kick his face in!"

"Oh, stop pretending to be stupid. You know damn well it wasn't Ottoline; what are you trying to do, play Watson?"

"Oh, thought you might enjoy setting me straight. I keep forgetting you don't like playing the Sherlock game."

"Well, try to remember. Seriously, can you imagine Ottoline doing anything so dumb? It just shows you that Borg may be a smart cookie in business, wheeling and dealing and assorted bullshit, but when it comes to the rough stuff he's a babe. He was trying to be clever and it backfired."

"Yeah, and it certainly confirms our suspicions of him."

"Suspicions! Well, I guess they were only suspicions, although I would put it stronger than that. But yes, what he has done now is made it a certainty. That helps. And you know where I saw Ed before? In a security-guard uniform at Universal Shoe."

"Oh great! Are you going to tell Ottoline about this little episode?"

"You call it 'a little episode'! It wasn't you that got bounced around. No, I don't think so. He's nervous about Borg pointing the finger at him as it is. What he doesn't know won't hurt any of us."

"So you don't tell him everything. I thought the two of you

were such buddies."

"Buddies, shmuddies. I don't tell anyone everything. I operate strictly on the principle of 'need to know'. Learned that much in the Navy. It's better that way."

"So what else haven't you told him?"

"You know damn well I wouldn't tell him about the bank statement Borg showed me!"

"What bank statement? Hey, you've been holding out on me, too!"

"Didn't I tell you? Sorry. At our last meeting in High Park Borg showed me his July bank statement. On Friday, July 23, he had withdrawn $6,000 in cash. He also showed me a receipt for $700 cash for a filly he bought at an auction the next day. Then he redeposited $300 on Tuesday. Neat, eh?"

"And that leaves ...."

"Five thousand unaccounted for. Which he said he gave to Martin."

"And since we know he didn't buy off Martin, he must still have that $5,000."

"Exactly. There is $5,000 in cash somewhere."

"What could he have done with it, that's the question."

"That's the question indeed."

"If we could find it, his story is blown. We would have him!"

"We would have $5,000, that's what we'd have."

"What the hell do you mean?"

"Nothing, nothing. You've been working in the straight world too long, Alex. Your healthy larcenous instincts are atrophying."

"Not a chance with you around."

So we spent the rest of Sunday rapping back and forth, guessing where Borg would be likely to stash five big ones. A really smart man would have destroyed them, but we did not think Borg would be psychologically capable of that. Murder, yes, but destroying money? No! Other possibilities we came up with were a bank account in another bank, another name; safety deposit ditto; hiding place at one of his three residences. He certainly couldn't have spent it, or given it away. Hard to spend an extra $5,000 cash in a couple of months without it showing. It would have to disappear. But a badly frightened man would want it accessible as getaway money. So where would he put it?

By suppertime we had exhausted the subject. Then we settled down for the evening, drinking beer and watching TV. The good Stock Ale went down well; the TV schedule was not too bad for once. I always like Alex's place, comfortable and uncluttered. Furniture painstakingly acquired over the years from auction sales, the Sally Ann, Crippled Civilians, now Americanized to "Goodwill Services". And the place was not as full of plants as some I know. Too much living matter sprouting from all directions can be disconcerting.

I fully intended to go to bed early, after the 11 o'clock news, get a good rest, and be up at 5:30 to make my breakfast appointment with Borg at the farm next morning. But it didn't work out that way.

The call came just before the 11 o'clock news. Alex answered. Thirty seconds later she walked back into the living room and motioned me to the phone extension in her bedroom.

"It's McPherson. I wonder what he wants this time."

"Probably to tell me he saw Martin on that Saturday, July 24, going to the Borgs'." I couldn't resist saying it, hoping I was right.

I had been thinking about Don's part in all this and had concluded that he must know something quite specific, which he was keeping to himself, hoping to turn it into cash.

McPherson's voice was subdued and anxious.

"Helen, Helen, I must talk to you. Now, right now. I'm scared, dead scared. I think I've done something very dumb. Hell, I *know* I have. Please, can you come over tonight? I must see you right away."

"Okay, I'm on my way. But first, if you've done what I suspect you've done, I suggest you be very, very careful until I get there. Keep your doors closed, don't go out, stay away from windows."

"Oh my god. Yes, yes, but hurry."

"Where is Katherine?"

"Right here with me. I told her everything. She persuaded me to call you. She's right. Please get here quick!"

"Should be around midnight. You'll recognize the truck. Hold on."

I dressed at top speed while Alex watched me. I told her what was happening.

"If it's dangerous for him, it's dangerous for you. What do you think he's done?"

"Sure it's dangerous. Probably tried to pressure Borg. I'll be armed just in case."

"I didn't know you carried a gun!"

"I don't carry it, but I have one in the truck."

"The Police Commission would not like that."

"Fuck the Police Commission."

"Tut, tut, such language. You must be nervous."

"Of course I'm nervous, dummy."

"I thought you had nerves of steel," she went on, teasing to ease the tension.

"Only automatons have nerves of steel. Having no nerves is a good way to get hurt. I need the adrenalin to keep me on my toes."

"It's a tough way to make a living."

"Tell me about it. Bye."

"What do I do if you don't come back?"

"Tonight you mean? I don't intend to come back tonight. Visiting Borg tomorrow, remember? I'll stay around and surprise him in the morning. I wonder if he's an early riser?"

"Be serious. No, really, what are you going to do? And call me for christ's sake when it's over, Okay?"

"When what's over? Listen, Alex, I don't know what I'm going to do. How can I? It will depend on what Don has done or said. But I have an uneasy feeling he's blown my whole scam somehow. Well, no point discussing it. I'm on my way."

Neither of us said anything more. A quick hug and I was out

the door. The truck was where I had left it. The Sunday night streets were busy, people coming and going. I envied every one of them, yet would not have exchanged places with any.

I broke all the traffic rules getting out of town and on the way to Caledon.

17

THE HOUSE WAS DARK AND QUIET. Even the dog was nowhere to be seen. I drove the truck behind the barn, got my gun, a Smith & Wesson Model 59, 9 mm. Luger and a flashlight, and then set off circling the house. It was dark; the full moon had been exactly a week earlier I remembered. My first day in Toronto. It had all taken just a week and a day. I shone the flashlight into the kitchen window where I had seen the glow of a lighted cigarette. I pressed my face to the glass and rapped. Almost immediately the door opened.

"Come in, come in. We saw you arrive and wondered what happened when you didn't come in here immediately. Man, am I glad you're here."

"So you're sitting here in the dark. Just as well it's not Hallowe'en. For future reference remember that a lighted cigarette is a good target. Oh, hello Katherine."

"Hi. Glad to see you. Do you think it's safe to turn on the light? I want some coffee. How about you?"

"That depends on what Don's been up to. Yes, I'll have coffee. Let's just move away from the window. There doesn't seem to be anyone in the immediate vicinity, but it's too easy to hide in this dark. Well, Don?"

"Sit down. I've been a fool. Oh, what a fool! You were quite right about me, quite right. I hate being poor. I wanted to lay my hands on some real dough. But most of all I wanted to get back at Borg .... Oh, how I hate that man!"

"You aren't poor, just envious and greedy. But never mind. You wanted to get back at Borg .... Start at the beginning."

"Well, after you left the other night Katherine and I did not talk. She just went to bed without a word." He turned to her. "Why did you do that? You know I can't stand it."

"You would just have had a tantrum. But I'm sorry. Helen, I am sorry. If I had talked with Don then and got it all out of him, well, it might have been different. As it is ...."

"Okay, let's save the might-have-beens for your shrink. Go on, Don."

He continued: "You don't understand. I left early on Friday before Kath was up, went to town, and didn't get back until last night. Last night, is that right, Kath?"

"More like this morning, Sunday morning. He had been drinking."

"Yes, well. A binge. A real binge. I was ripped out of my skull for two days. Passed out in the car. Thank God it was parked. Came to, decided to go home. I don't know how I did it but I got here okay."

"He arrived, almost fell out of the car, and started babbling about what he would do to Henry Borg. I put him to bed and went back to my studio to work. I checked on him once during the day, aout 2 P.M., and he was sleeping like a lamb. Next time I looked, he was gone. Tell Helen what you did, Don."

"You won't spare me anything, will you. Well, confession is good for the soul. I woke up with a raging headache; I don't know what time it was. I felt sorry for myself, mad at the world, at Kath, at you, at myself, but mostly at Borg. So I had two or three quick ones to kill the pain."

"Two or three! More like half a bottle of scotch, that's what you had!"

"Details! But yes, it was a lot on top of what I had. And it hit me. You know how hazy you can get; drinking two days, little sleep, more booze, all the bad vibes and years of hate churning in you. So I got my pants on, walked out of the house, and went to see Henry next door. You know his place? Well, he was in the back room downstairs he calls his study. The French windows were closed but not locked. So I walked in and surprised him."

"This is getting more and more like a bad English murder mystery told from the point of view of the murderer. What did you hit him with?"

"No, no. It's not like that at all! Hell, if I had killed him I wouldn't have to worry about him trying to get me. No, I just raved at him for half an hour. He gave me a drink, and tried to make sense of what I was saying."

"The suspense is making me itch. What were you saying? You hate to admit it even now, don't you?"

"I said a great many things, going back to the 'good old days' in London. But what really matters is that I told him I knew about Martin and Oscar and that I had seen Martin on a Saturday evening in July walking past our drive towards his."

"Well, that's not so compromising. He now admits Martin came to see him."

"Ah, but he didn't admit it to me. He asked me how I could be sure it was Martin; there are occasional hitchhikers on our road. So I told him that I recognized him and we spoke. I was surprised that he was going on rather than coming in to see Katherine. He said he was going to see Henry and would drop in on his way back to do his laundry here. He had all his duds with him, pack and guitar, everything."

This was bad news. Henry's story was falling apart, just when I wanted him to feel safe about it. He had definitely stated that Martin did not have his things with him when he arrived. That was foolish but Henry was now committed to it. The disappearance of the gear was one of the things he was using to point to Ottoline. Now that was gone.

"Why didn't Martin just leave his things here and go on without them?"

"He didn't want to stay and talk. He had not wanted to be seen; it was an accident I saw him. I think he intended to arrive later and have us assume he had just gotten here from Toronto. He hitchhiked of course, and had to walk from the highway."

At this point Katherine broke in.

"I don't know what it all means but it meant a lot to Henry. He tried to kill Don."

"Yes, this is the part you'll like. He tried to drown me in his pool! Really, I'm not kidding! He pushed me outside the French doors, grabbed me by the hair, and tried to trip me right into the water! I couldn't believe it."

"I believe it. How come he didn't succeed?"

"Is that all you have to say? Oh, 'luck of the drunk', I guess. Just then that man of his, what's his name ....?"

"Jerry Sharpe."

"Jerry Sharpe, yes; how did you know? Anyway he appeared. Or rather we heard him and it distracted Henry so I shook him off and ran. Oh, man, did I run! Scratches all over me. See?"

"Small price. So then what happened?"

"Nothing. I just got back here. Katherine was looking for me so I told her the whole thing."

"You tell her you had sent Gale Mangoni to pump Oscar?"

Don looked put out.

"No, I hadn't mentioned that .... but what does that matter? He tried to kill me! That proves he killed Martin."

"Not in a court of law, it doesn't. You were drunk; you could have tripped."

"Yes, but we can be morally certain."

"We're already morally certain. All you've done is spooked him, but good. And that blows my scam. Oh well, perhaps it wasn't so good anyway."

"What scam? What do we do now?"

"You and Kath are going to bed. I'll visit Mr. Borg, see if he too is taking his rest. Right to bed now. Sleep it off, both of you. You look like you need it."

Katherine spoke up.

"I don't understand any of it. What spooked Henry so much? And why does it bother you?"

"Everything about Henry bothers me. He has done a lot of very dumb things, but nothing quite damaging enough to get him. We still don't know what happened to Martin."

"Maybe he's still alive? Oh, please God ...."

"No , Katherine, that's one thing for sure. Don't keep on hoping, it's useless. Go to bed, close all the doors. I'll sleep in the truck. 'Night."

I stayed in the dark kitchen while they stumbled their way

up to bed. I checked around the house again. What would Borg do now? He was definitely losing his grip, he was scared. But in fact if he kept his nerve none of this added up to much more than a 'moral certainty'. Moral certainty and a dime are still only a dime and a dime won't get you anything. Without the body. And that was probably at the bottom of Georgian Bay, impossible to find without Borg's help, and since his plot to frame Ottoline had just lost a strand he was not likely to let it turn up. Where did that leave me? Pushing, that's where. Which was dangerous. Like Alex said, it's a tough way to make a living.

Would he make another attempt to cool Don? And Katherine too? My instinct said no, but considering the risk, I couldn't bet on it. So I got into the pickup and drove the quarter-mile to the Borg gate. It was closed as I expected. I parked on the side, careful of the deep ditch, climbed the gate, and walked as quietly as I could towards the main house, the gun quite comfortable at the back of my waistband.

No lights, no sound. I checked the pool area, the change shack, the door to the study was locked. Then the front of the house, all doors and windows. All secure. Then the garage. Only one car, a newish Oldsmobile. I checked everything over quite thoroughly — the garage, the car trunk. Satisfied, I left everything where it was and called it a night.

18

IT WAS 6:45 BY MY DASHBOARD CLOCK when I let myself out of the truck parked well out of sight behind Payne's barn studio. Katherine was already in the kitchen making coffee again. She was tousled, red-eyed and non-communicative.

"Want some breakfast?" she asked.

"Just coffee. I'm expected for breakfast at Mr. Borg's. Hope it's pancakes."

"Oh, for god's sake, stop it! This super cool number is too much to take on an empty stomach. Now I wish I had called the whole thing off while I had the chance. Martin is dead, what else matters?"

"At least I'm glad you realize that it can't be called off anymore."

"Do you think Henry really tried to kill Don? Or was Don just hallucinating? He didn't appear to have been followed. You didn't find any signs of Henry skulking about, did you?"

"No, I didn't. And the facts about that attempt hardly matter. It could be that Henry first panicked and then reconsidered. He doesn't like Don either, does he? And had every reason to get mad at him. Once Don was gone, he could have cooled down and done some heavy thinking. He doesn't really have anything to worry about if he keeps his head."

"So where does all this get us? It was all a silly false alarm. Is that what you're saying."

"No. I'm not saying that. What happened between those two is important. Which is why I'm going to see Henry now pretending I know nothing of it. Just one more way to get and keep him off balance. He will have to decide how much to tell me. What attitude would an innocent man take? Difficult for him."

"Is that how it's done? Keep people off balance, pretend you don't know what you do know?"

"Yes, and pretend to know what you don't know. That's how

it's done."

"Well, I hope you enjoy your breakfast with Henry." Katherine did not sound friendly. Just as well I had not set out to be universally loved.

I finished my coffee, went to the pickup, and drove to Henry's. It was 7:15.

First person I saw was Molly Sharpe in riding boots, leading a horse out of the stables. She waved and waited until she saw that I was stopping by the big house. Then she went on, missing my waved greeting.

Henry was at the door. He was half-dressed; no coat or shoes. Looking peaked. He was gracious.

"My, you are prompt. Very prompt. Good. Breakfast will be ready right away. I am baching it, of course, so you'll have to put up with my cooking. My wife went back to town yesterday. Some meeting or other. Come in, come in."

I came in. He was looking at me out of the corner of his eyes. Looking for bruises, perhaps. Or just gauging my attitude. I did have a bruise on my temple but my attitude was not showing much. I said nothing. Wiped my feet and walked in.

We went into the kitchen, all pine, droves of color-matched appliances and expensive equipment for the pampered kitchen. Very nice.

There was a jug of juice on the table, drip coffee in an automatic coffee maker, eggs and bacon all prepared by the stove. But no pancakes.

"You eat bacon and eggs, I hope? It's all I have. Good. Get the bread, will you? It's in the breadbox, see, over there." He waved his arm and turned to the frypan. Very civilized. No hint of anger or concern. You would never think there had been a cross word between us. I still had not said a word. Instead, I got the bread, whole wheat, buttered a couple of slices. Sat down, poured out the juice, and stared out the window, sipping.

"Ah, you too have trouble getting it together in the morning. I hate morning people. Always takes me some time to wake up. But you must have gotten up early to get here by this time.

Did you drop in next door by any chance?"

Chatter, chatter. He couldn't stand the silence. So he was fishing.

"Bit early for unannounced visitors," I said.

"But I understand Katherine is an early riser."

"Yes, she was up. But Don wasn't. He had a bad night, she told me. Been drinking all weekend."

"So you did stop off there! As for Don drinking, well, that's nothing new. He really is a menace when he's soused. Do you know, he visited here yesterday, dead drunk, yelling obscenities? Had to chase him out. That man should be committed. Dry out somewhere."

So that was his story. No word about Don seeing Martin and the pack which was not there. I let it ride.

"Here's your B and Es. If you want toast just pop it in there. And coffee; you know these things really make good coffee. And no trouble. Well worth the money."

Finally he sat down, buttered, poured, salt-and-peppered, bit. We ate in silence, hungrily. Once he got up to get me some honey. I poured us more coffee.

When we were through eating he pushed aside his plate, put both arms on the table, and leaned towards me.

"Now what did you come here to see?"

"I want a replay of the time Martin came to see you. Saturday, July 24, evening I believe."

"A replay? How do you mean?"

"What was said and done where. Where Martin stood, where you were throughout. It shouldn't be difficult. Once you begin with where you first saw him, just go over what happened step by step."

"Why? I still don't see why."

"Never mind why. Just do it."

"Okay. I said I would so I will. Well, he just walked up the drive. I saw him before he reached the door."

"How was he dressed? What did he have with him?"

"I can't remember exactly. What he usually wore, I guess.

Jeans and a fancy shirt."

"And he definitely did not have his pack with him? You're still sure of that? Think, remember, see him walking up the drive — does he have a pack and guitar? Or not? Think, man, think."

Silence.

"I am thinking. He definitely had no gear with him, just the clothes he stood in. I'm sure of that much."

I decided to let it go for the time being. There would be an opportunity to hit him with Don's story later.

"Go on," I said. Relieved that that hurdle was over, he continued.

"So we said hello and went into my study. We sat down, I gave him a drink ...."

"What drink? And how about you? Didn't you have anything?"

"A beer, Martin drank beer. And yes, I had a scotch and water. That's what I usually drink."

"So there you were nice and cozy, having a man-to-man talk about Oscar's fair white body. Right."

"Look here! I let you into my house; I'm co-operating as best I can. I must insist you keep a civil tongue in your head."

"Just go on talking. Never mind my tongue. Then what?"

So we went over his story again and again. Most of the action took place in the study — discussion of Oscar, the offer of $5,000, and according to Henry, Martin's acceptance. Then, again according to Henry, Martin just picked up and left. Walked away down the drive to catch a lift into town. All through this very straightforward narrative I needled him with nasty comments and uncomfortable questions. Like:

"So here it is the middle of July and you don't even go onto the terrace and sit by the pool? It must have been a long hot trip for Martin. How come you didn't offer him a swim?"

"Oh, I forgot. He did go into the pool. Just to cool off. Not for long."

"So what else did you forget? How come the Sharpes didn't see him come or go?"

"The Sharpes? How do you know them? Have you been questioning my help behind my back? What did they say?"

"Well, for one, they heard someone in the pool. Just as well you 'remembered' about that swim. You know, for a businessman you're a bad liar. Now let's get the sequence right this time. At what point in the proceedings did this cooling dip take place?"

And back he had to go, trying to make it all sound reasonable. He was no longer so affable but did manage to keep himself under control.

"Interesting. So this swim was the last thing Martin did. Before he left I mean. That's right, is it? You were all palsy-walsy; he had his five Gs and you had his promise to keep away from Oscar. That's right, is it? So you offered him use of your pool. Just like that. Strange timing under the circumstances, don't you think?"

"I don't care what you think! That's what happened!"

"So here is Martin, $5,000 richer, going back to town the same night he arrived. Kind of strange, don't you think?"

"Why strange? He just went home."

"But he didn't go 'home'. Not to either of them. He didn't go back to Nate's. He didn't drop by to se his mother. Surprising, eh? Here he was, obviously tired, hot and hungry. It was evening; why didn't he stay at his mother's that night?"

"He told me he didn't want to bother her, that she would ask questions."

"Funny. Don says Martin told him he intended to see his mother and do his laundry .... after he saw you."

"Don says! What Don says isn't worth a nickel. He would say anything to embarrass me. I told you he is a menace. What else did he tell you?"

"That he saw Martin arrive carrying all his gear. And why should he lie about that?"

"I don't know. When did he tell you all this?"

"Last night. And I think Don could sue you for defamation of character, and probably attempted murder. You know Henry, it really would be nice if your story made sense. I had hoped you had this thing more together. As it is, it will be the devil's own job to keep you from being more than embarrassed. Perhaps it's time we took off for the cottage. Unless you have anything here to tell me or show me."

"You really are insufferable. Okay, let's go."

We walked out in silence and got into his car. Neither of us spoke while Borg navigated the various concession roads and until we got onto the 400 north. Borg was mulling something over in his mind and I left him to it. It was a pleasant fall day; I relaxed and enjoyed the ride. Even under strain, Borg was a good driver. The big Oldsmobile was quiet and comfortable. Finally he started the conversation again. Very carefully.

"I can understand, more or less, why you might want to see the farm and go over Martin's visit there. But there is no possible justification for this trip to our cottage."

I grinned at him.

"No, there isn't, is there? And yet here we are on our way. You are taking me there. And we both know why, don't we?"

This time I laughed out loud. He was silent for a good minute. Then:

"This cat-and-mouse game you think you're playing with me just won't work, you know. You may think what you like, but you have no proof, not anything solid that the police would look at. Now I've gathered that you're not stupid. No, indeed. So what is this all about?"

"Are you calling yourself a mouse, Henry? You're the cat — a fat cat. One of the things about fat cats is that they have a lot to lose. You have a lot to lose, Henry. You have money, position, a future, the envy of your friends, your son's respect .... everything you have built your life around. It doesn't take a trip to Kingston to lose all that. No sir. There is more than one way to skin a cat like you, Henry."

He had been holding his breath while I talked. He let it out slowly.

"Skin a cat like me. I see. I think I see. Okay, what do you want?"

"What's the hurry, Henry? Let's get to the cottage, look around, have a drink, maybe go for a boat ride. Lots of time, no hurry at all. Are you in a hurry, Henry? You should learn patience and fortitude. Even captains of industry need to learn patience and fortitude."

"This war of nerves is idiotic!" He could no longer restrain himself.

"Why don't you just drive, so I can enjoy the ride? We'll get down to business in good time."

He gritted his teeth and drove.

We took the road to Honey Harbour and from there a maze of cottage roads through the bush. It was close to noon when we finally arrived at the Borg cottage. The sun was making feeble attempts to shine; some of the leaves were off the trees. The cottage was locked but not yet closed up for the winter. Henry fumbled for a key and together we managed to get the back door opened. It was cold outside, and Henry turned on the space heater in the living room while I got the ready kindling going in the big fireplace. All this without a glance at each other. It was very quiet, no neighbors, and hardly the sound of a boat.

"Want a drink?" Henry asked.

"Yes, I'll have a brandy if you have any."

"Right." He disappeared into a walk-in pantry off the kitchen area and reappeared with a cardboard box full of bottles. The supply had been put away out of sight of the local prowlers. Now he proceeded to set up the bar again, wiping the bar counter, polishing glasses, picking the stirrers carefully. It was a familiar and comforting chore for him. He fixed himself a scotch and poured my brandy.

"We're lucky: the refrigerator isn't turned off yet. There is ice if you want it."

"No thanks."

By now the fire was going full blast. He handed me my drink and sat down gratefuly in front of the fireplace with his. I lifted up my glass in mock salute and looked around me at the large, well-furnished living room, the expanse of picture window overlooking the boathouse and the lake.

"Yes, Henry, you have a lot to lose."

"Why and how should I lose it? All your vague threats cut no ice with me. I know where I stand."

"Do you? If you really felt as secure as you pretend you would have thrown me out on my ear long ago. But you can't, because you need to know what I know, what I suspect, and especially what I intend to do. You need to know how well you've done. There is the story you're trying to make others believe, and then there is what really happened. You have gone over both so often in your mind you are no longer sure of either. You don't know when it's necessary to lie and when it's better to tell the truth. That's what happened with the story of Martin's gear. You tried to involve Ottoline in other ways too. It all backfired. Now you're not sure how much damage was done."

Here I paused, giving him a chance to step in. He didn't, so I continued.

"Just look at it, Henry, look. You told Oscar not to talk to me, you tried to bribe me, you lied about Martin's gear. Two nights ago you tried to have me put out of action by two hope-lessly inept dudes, you scared Don out of his wits ...."

Now he interrupted.

"What do you mean I tried to put you out of action? You can't tie me to that! It must have been Ottoline. I told you he was a gangster!"

"Henry, wake up! Ed Wintermans is a security guard at Universal Shoe! If Ottoline wanted to put me away he would most likely have succeeded. Precisely because he is a 'gang-ster', as you put it. Let's drop that pretence or we won't get anywhere."

"All right, all right, I admit I've been stupid, I admit I have something to protect. My son's good name, his future, my repu-tation ...."

"Well, that's a start. Lies are one thing, but having someone beat up is not merely criminal, it's stupid. The weakness of your outraged father scenario is that if it constitutes a reason for your stupidity, it also constitutes a motive for murder."

"Motive. I may have had a motive but that doesn't mean I killed Martin."

"Motive is just one part of it. WIth all the lies and attempts at a frame, there's one thing you can't get away from: Martin was last seen at your place in your company. He was never seen again! Neither he nor his gear were ever seen again. Or heard from. You killed him. There is no other explanation. Get that through your head! You had means and opportunity. Together with this motive, which you yourself admit is strong, it makes you the killer. All your subsequent attempts to distract attention from these facts only made things worse. Wise up. It's much too late for denials. We have to deal with what really happened. I think I know most of it already."

"What do you know? You haven't got a body!"

That last just slipped out. It amounted to a confession. Psychologically he had dropped his defenses. My strategy was working well so far. The next step was tricky, but I felt pretty confident. I did not believe he could establish another line of defense at this point. His only cover was blown, so I pressed my advantage.

"With or without a body, you've had it. Listen. You killed Martin at the farm. Drowned him in the pool. You probably hit him or held him down. You knew an accident story wouldn't wash. So you packed him into the trunk of your car, the same car that's standing out there now, the Olds, and brought him here to the lake. After your wife and son left on Monday for Montreal you took the body out in your boat and dumped it in the lake. Probably weighted down. Where is it, Henry?"

"No, no! It was an accident. But I knew no one would believe me. Oscar would not believe me, he knew how I felt, so I had to get rid of the body. The lake semed the best place. It was an accident, he hit his head diving ...."

"Nuts. Of course no one would believe it then, so why should

I believe it now? And disposing of the body here makes it murder for sure. It doesn't matter what really happened at the pool. Let's not kid around any more. Where is it? Show me."

"Why should I show you? Without a body there's no case!"

"Henry, Henry. I don't need a case to stand up in court. I can blow your life sky high without it! If you haven't seen that yet, it's time you did. Why do you think we're here?"

"Why? I don't know. Except that you think I'll show you where his body is. Why should I?"

"Because .... what's the alternative?"

"That's not an alternative! Regardless of what you know, that would just make things worse for me!"

"Not necessarily."

That gave him pause. And no wonder. He stopped to consider the implications. I helped him along the line of thought I wanted him to follow.

"As things are, you're over a barrel. If you don't co-operate with me, I'll destroy you. That's a certainty. So why not consider other possibilities?"

I hoped he was not going to be too dense in his distraught state. One more prompt seemed necessary.

"Remember what I said in the car? 'There is more than one way to skin a cat.' Remember?"

He swallowed it. No choice, really.

"I already offered you $10,000. You didn't take it. How much do you want?"

"I didn't know enough about what the bribe was for. First rule in taking a payoff is to know what you're being paid off for! Don't you even know that? It's just common sense. It's dangerous not to know."

"I see. Blackmail, pure and simple. How much?"

"Hardly pure and simple. The situation of a blackmailer is very sensitive. Unless one holds all the cards it's too much of a risk. Dig?"

"How much?"

"Henry, you're not listening. Once I accept your money for

keeping my mouth shut, I am accessory after the fact to murder. Therefore, I must know as much as you do or you have the upper hand. It is also in your interest that I be fully involved. We become accomplices. If one of us falls, so does the other. That's the only safety for either of us. Now do you understand?"

Now he understood. He looked at me as if I was a monster.

"I never thought of it that way. But you're right, of course. Man, what a mind you must have."

It was fun to see the enormity of what I had suggested hit him. He immediately felt morally superior.

"Okay, let's deal. How much?"

This he understood. Buying and selling. He had the money; I wanted it. That gave him control. He never considered what was being sold.

"First I'll take that $5,000 in cash that Martin didn't get. It's written off already, right? And it's in your car where you've been hiding it. Then we'll take a boat ride."

"How the hell could you know it's in the car? Okay, okay, you can have it. Glad to get rid of it, really. It's been a problem, you know."

Now that we were partners, he was taking me into his confidence.

"A lucky guess," I lied. "The best place under the circumstances. And the Sharpes mentioned as one of your recent idiosyncrasies that you insisted on using and servicing the Olds yourself. Now let's get it."

We went out of the cottage almost arm in arm. Henry was close to being cheerful. I may be a devious woman, but I could be bought, which made me fully comprehensible, he was thinking. The money, in $100-bills, was shoved into an old inner tube and spread flat under the rubber mat in the trunk of the car. I had found it there the previous night. What a hiding place. What anyone would make of the presence of an inner tube in a car with modern steel radials I couldn't imagine. But then that was Borg all over. Clever, but not clever enough. Since I did not have my truck with me I merely counted the money and put it back. It was still safer than having it on me.

"I'll take the car keys." He handed them to me, pointing out the trunk key, which I did not need.

"Right, now it's yours. Give me a hand getting the boat out. Glad I haven't drained the motor yet. Should have enough gas left to get us there and back. Wouldn't want to have to swim in this temperature."

Joke. I couldn't believe he thought his worries were over. No, it was just the partial relief from the tension, the fresh air, and the two stiff drinks which were talking. He was nervous. Well, I was not exactly relaxed either.

The boat was an 18-foot Grew with a 164-horsepower Mercury engine. Ugly plastic. Like an oceangoing bathtub. Fast: to make a big wake, outrun the neighbors, and tow water-skiers. I like canoes myself. Henry checked the boat over meticulously, adjusted the windscreen, side curtains; handed me a D.O.T.-approved life preserver; turned on the engine and listened to it while it roared and sputtered. Finally satisfied, he motioned me to sit down in the vinyl-covered chair to his left. We were off.

"A nice fall day for a boat ride," Henry said. "Do you know Georgian Bay at all? It's great country, gorgeous."

"Really. I've been around here before but not at this time of year. Yeah, it's pleasant. But it's too open and full of motorboats for canoeing. I prefer the smaller lake chains, with no cottages and only a few fishing boats."

"You're one of those hardy outdoor types. I thought so. We're pretty civilized out here. That's what I like, all the comforts of the city with outdoor fun on your doorstep."

"Yeah, just like the beer ads," I said.

He laughed. "Something like that."

There was a weird quality to our conversation. We were supposedly on our way to the spot where Borg had dumped Martin's body and here we were chatting like a couple of weekend cottagers. Henry felt good behind the wheel of his boat. He was in control again. Something had clicked in that ugly mind of his. I had a good idea what that might be. Now that I was revealed as a blackmailer, he could kill me with a clear conscience. Isn't that all that blackmailers deserved? It was the situation with Martin all over again. It was okay to dispose of people who threatened him and who were, in his estimation, evil. He would not ever think of killing a business rival, but fags and blackmailers were fair game. The difference was that moral superiority which he needed to feel. He could do anything in his righteousness.

Since I had deliberately brought about this situation, I would have only myself to blame if things went his way. And knowing that I had read him correctly and that my so-called plan was working did not bring me any comfort at that moment. Perhaps it's better to die in the knowledge that one was right, but it seems poor consolation for being dead. I had no intention of turning up dead. The problem was how to prevent it.

Henry Borg was an adult male with two stiff drinks inside him, in charge of his own boat and on his own lake. It's true that I had a life-preserver on and he had not, but since he had arranged it that way it was obviously not an impediment to whatever he intended. It's also true that I had a gun. I didn't think he had one on him. I had seen him without a coat and he had not been out of my sight since — except in the pantry. Yes, he might have had a gun hidden there. But on the whole, it was unlikely. Canadian businessmen do not by and large own handguns at all and if they do they don't keep them in their summer cottages. A rifle, yes; handgun, no. Still, it was a possibility not to be completely discounted. What else? The simplest method would be the best. Hit me over the head with something, a paddle perhaps. There was one clipped under the lefthand gunwale, all according to D.O.T. boat safety regulations. Could he reach it without leaving his seat? Could I? No, to both. A tool of some kind? There was nothing within easy reach. The boat was clean and empty except for some fishing gear stowed at the back. I decided to quit that line of reasoning and concentrate on what he was doing. That was interessting enough.

Borg had taken the boat straight out into the lake; we had

passed between two islands and seemed to be moving in a large curve across an expanse of open water. There was no way he would try anything in sight of the mainland or any of the island cottages. It was daylight and even though we had not seen any other boats, on a Monday in October there were sure to be people on shore. It had also been a Monday when he dumped Martin's body. And in July Georgian Bay is full of boats and cottagers. So he knew of a place which was unfrequented and not overlooked from anywhere. I had counted on that in maneuvering the situation to this point. But there was not much to be said for finding Martin's body by joining it at the bottom of the lake.

We passed another larger island and entered a narrow channel between it and a low outcrop of rock with only a few stunted trees. The boat slowed down: there were rocks just under the water; buoys marked the safe passage between them. Just as we were about to come out from behind the large island, the motor sputtered. Henry cursed — too cheerfully, somehow — and spun the wheel. The boat turned; the motor died; the bow rammed gently onto a small sandy beach between some rocks. Very fortunate.

"Shit," said Henry. "Oh, I beg your pardon. Such language in front of a lady! Sorry. This engine needs an overhaul. Must be dirt in the gas line. Never mind, soon fix it!" His excitement was evident, understandable .... and horrifying!

He moved to the stern and yanked the outboard motor up until it came out of the water. He fiddled with it, his back to me, hiding what he was doing. Then he turned, a broad smile on his face, and said:

"Would you mind coming back here? We're aground, and shifting your weight might lift the bow. Then we can get going again."

So that was it. I stood up awkwardly and moved along holding onto the gunwale, in a little crouch as if unsure of my footing. We acted simultaneously and in a split second he swung at me with a fish billy and I hit out with the paddle which I had grabbed when I saw him move. It was all over in a moment. My blow connected solidly, sending him over the stern; I stood and nursed a bruised arm. Carefully I move over and looked down. He was unconscious but still buoyant, his face submerged. As I watched, the weight of his waterlogged clothes dragged him down a little farther. Left that way he would be dead in minutes. It was a temptation to let him die. But there were too many things I still didn't know. Or maybe it just wasn't my day to play God.

It took a bit of doing to pull him ashore, take off his jacket, and push the water out of his lungs. Finally he gasped and spluttered, helpless but alive. Lying there wet, face down on the Precambrian rock, Henry did not look the self-righteous patriarch. Just a stupid slob who had taken on more than he could handle. But I knew that as his breath returned and his fear receded he would be back to his 'normal', dangerous self. Now was my best chance to get at the truth — as he knew it.

"Where is it, Henry? Where's Martin's body? Speak up man, unless you want to join him."

"On the other side, under that rock face. It's deep and there are rocks down there. There was a slide. I wedged him in .... You need scuba gear ...." He gasped.

"Okay. And speaking of gear, is his gear there too?"

He coughed, his face red.

"I told you, I told you the truth. He didn't have his gear with him. You must believe me. Don lied .... and I didn't kill him, I didn't!"

"You mean it really was an accident? And you went to all this trouble to make it look like murder? That's crazy!"

"Let me sit up. I'll tell you. I may as well. It's such an unbelievable story. But I swear it's the truth. I swear! Help me sit up."

"Okay, sit up. Here, lean against this rock. No tricks now. You're in no shape to take me on."

"I know it. How come you didn't let me drown. Oh, my god, I feel sick ...." And he was.

There was nothing for it but to watch him throw up and wait

until he was able to talk again. I had to keep the pressure on.

"Don't get too comfortable. Just talk."

"Oh, I wish I hadn't had those two drinks at the cottage. And it's so cold. God, that was close ...."

"Never mind feeling sorry for yourself. Talk! Tell me this 'unbelievable' story."

"Well, most of it was just as I told you. Martin agreed to go away. He took my money, signed a receipt. Then he laughed and went to take a dip in the pool."

Henry stopped and wiped his face; he was drooling.

"He took your bribe?" I repeated stupidly.

"Yes, yes. How else do you think I got that receipt?"

"Forgery is not unknown."

"No. He signed it."

"So it all went as you planned."

"Yes." He paused, but this time in order to say something which surprised even him. "But I was angry. It proved he didn't care for Oscar. God, how I hated him. It was all a lark to him. Not important. My son throwing his life away on a heartless faggot! God!"

"So?"

"Well, he went into the pool and .... here, let me rest a bit. It's hard to talk so much."

"Hard or not, go on man. We're just getting to the good part." I was firm. No intention of letting him get off the hook now.

"All right, all right. Where was I? Ah, yes. I went to the kitchen to get more ice, had a leak, then went upstairs and generally tried to calm down so I could bear to see him again. I had another drink and sort of got a grip on myself." He paused again.

"Yes, go on."

He went on quickly, the words spilling out of his mouth.

"When I walked out to the poolside Martin was dead in the water. Dead! I don't know what happened! Really, I don't know!"

"Henry! You're putting me on! You went away and he drowned before you got back. Oh, come on."

"Yes, yes, I know. I knew no one would believe me. Oscar certainly wouldn't. It was Oscar I was worried about. If he arrived just then and found me with Martin's body .... well, I would lose him. Do you see why I had to do what I did? No matter how it would look, even if I was found out later? I know it looks like murder, I know. But I had to hide Martin's body. Oscar ...."

"What do you mean if Oscar arrived just then? Wasn't he up at the cottage? Hadn't he left just that morning?"

"Oh, I guess I hadn't mentioned that Oscar had called from the cottage. He insisted on coming back to the farm to see Martin, so I thought he was on his way. You see the spot I was in? As it turned out he changed his mind part way down but I didn't know that at the time ...."

I admit I was stunned.

"Just a cotton-picking minute. Why hasn't anyone mentioned this before? When was this call?"

"It didn't seem to matter, since he never got there. And there were two calls: The first one from the cottage just before Martin got to the farm. Oscar, upset, wanting to know what I intended, insisting on speaking to Martin in person. And the second .... after Martin was dead. From somewhere on the highway. The wagon needed gassing up so he called from a service station. He wanted to know what was happening, couldn't wait to find out how Martin had reacted. I told him Martin had already left. I lied; I had to. So he just went back. Didn't bother showing up. That's all. But when I found Martin's body, I didn't know that Oscar would call from the road. I expected him to arrive momentarily. So I took Marin's body, wrapped it in an old horse blanket together with his clothes, and put it in the trunk of the Olds."

"Why didn't you tell Oscar what really happened? How come you didn't trust him to believe you? Your beloved son! You could have replaced the body in the pool, called a doctor, the police .... Did what an innocent man would have done."

Now he was shouting:

"*My* beloved son, as you put it, had just had a homosexual relationship. And did not trust me .... right? How could I trust him, his feelings for Martin? I couldn't take that chance! Anyway, it was too late. The Sharpes were back by then. I couldn't take the risk of being seen moving the body again. Anyway, it seemed the best thing to do. Best all around, for everybody. Martin would just disappear ...."

"The timing. How long did all this take? How long between the first call and the second? What time was Oscar's second call?"

"Hard to say exactly. Between 8:30 and 10:00 or so would be my guess. Hour and a half, two hours. From Oscar's first call, just before Martin arrived, to when he phoned from the Gulf Station on the 400 ...."

"You mean the Sharpes were back by 10 P.M.? On a Saturday night?"

"Well, maybe 10:30. And yes, I heard their car. They have a little Datsun pickup. It's unmistakable, the noise it makes. They were back. Maybe they quarreled or just decided on an early night."

"And Martin's gear. You're sure he didn't have it with him when he arrived?"

"I'm absolutely sure."

I made him go over it all again. And again. More details. But his story remained the same. Martin had accepted the $5,000. He had not killed Martin. He hid the body because no one would have believed it had been an accident and he was expecting Oscar to walk in at any moment. There was no gear. And Oscar had called twice: before Martin arrived and again after he was dead. The Sharpes were home early so he couldn't undo what he had done with Martin's body. He did not budge from any of it. No amount of badgering would make him.

19

I GOT US BACK TO THE COTTAGE, Henry sitting bundled in the bottom of the boat, teeth chattering. Even after a rubdown and some dry cottage clothes, he did not appear to be back to normal. Guess the shock of having the tables turned on him, not to mention facing death, was having long-term effects.

So I drove the Olds to the Caledon farm. Except to ask me what I intended to do about Martin's body, Henry was silent all the way. I was glad of that. My mind was too busy for conversation. Martin's body could stay where it was for a while: the lake wouldn't freeze for a month or so yet. What was occupying my attention, of course, were the implications of what Henry had told me about that strange evening of July 24. I needed time to think them through. And to decide what to do next.

Actually that was easy. Once at the farm I saw Henry into bed with a couple of sleeping pills and a large dose of whiskey, and called Alex. She was home, impatient to hear from me. I told her. We discussed Henry's revelations.

"It could be true, you know. I can sort of believe it and understand why Henry disposed of the body, even if he hadn't killed Martin," I said at one point.

"Yeah, could be. But what about this bit about Oscar phoning and then not arriving? And Martin accepting the bread? What's your reading on that?"

"Well, you know, I'm getting quite different vibes about the whole scene now. It does give this affair a new perspective. It's not as simple as we originally thought."

"You mean there could have been some plot between Martin and Oscar? To rip off Henry for five Gs?" Alex is quick.

"Something like that. Will have to work it out. See how it fits."

"And how about the discrepancy about Martin's gear? Which one is lying, Don or Henry? Or neither?"

"What's your guess?"

"I suspect neither. Which means that Martin disposed of his gear between the time Don met him on the road and Henry saw him walking up to his door. But where, and why?"

"That's the question. It could be simply that he was tired and hot and thought that since he wouldn't be at Henry's long he could just put his gear down somewhere and pick it up later. Remember, it was summer. And a good mile hike from the road."

"Or?" asked Alex.

"He met someone in that last eighth of a mile who took care of his gear."

"Katherine!"

"Could be. Taking care of her son's stuff. All the dirty laundry Martin was supposed to have. Could be."

"Why? Why didn't she say she had seen him? Why keep it dark?"

"Who knows? Maybe it wasn't her. Maybe it was someone else. Maybe he just left it in the bush."

"In which case it would either still be there, or someone has found it but has said nothing."

"Anyone could have found it. Passing hiker. Local kids. Hunters. There was an expensive guitar. Worth stealing."

"But still .... are you saying the disappearing gear is not relevant? Do you seriously believe Martin's death was accidental, just a fluke? And that there is no mystery and there would not be any if Henry had not tried to hide the body?"

"Alex, I honestly don't know. Such a complex set of circumstances. So much emotional stress. All just a coincidence? Possible, but not probable."

"Look, probability is a tricky thing, right? Anything which can happen, will. Perhaps seldom, but it will. The one-in-a-million shot can come in."

"Yes, of course, but I prefer to proceed with the odds. Especially when there is a convenient death involved. Coincidence be damned! I don't believe it."

"A hunch again, Helen?"

"Yeah, a hunch. Want to make something of it?"

"Nope. Carry on. Your hunches are usually good, that I'll admit. So what happens now?"

"Now? I go after Oscar. And Katherine and Don and the Sharpes. You check on those phone calls, check pawnshops for that guitar. Get Nate to give you the details on it. He'll know. Come on, come on. Let's get on with it! We just made $2,500 each. Let's earn it."

"Okay. Done. Look, how about Henry? Where is he at since his dunking? And Martin's body. You planning to fish it out?"

"Not until I'm satisfied what happened. What's the point? Henry will keep mum. I think he'll stay that way at least until something starts happening to that precious son of his. That Oscar! Wait till I get my hands on him! Never said a word about those phone calls."

"Poor Oscar. He sure held back on you."

"He told me as little as he could. Enough to get me off his back. It could be just the regular way he has of operating. Strategy of the weak. Now I have another wedge; he'll tell me more."

Alex was amused at my impatience. She is more a researcher, less a participant, than I am. Doesn't get as involved. Perhaps that's what comes of staying in the background, the back room, out of the action. Cause or effect? Doesn't matter. Fact is, she does have more distance, objectivity. Very useful. Thing is, she finds out and reports, but doesn't make things happen. And doesn't want to.

Where to start? Oscar seemed the most interesting, but he was in town while Don and the Sharpes were right there. Logistics dictated getting at them first.

20

So DON IT WAS. I called the farm next door and he answered.

"It's Helen. I'm at Henry's. I want to talk to you. Just walk over to the back of the house by the pool. Meet you there."

"What? What happened?"

"Never mind. I don't want to talk on the phone. Just show up immediately. Don't tell Katherine. Be here!"

"Okay okay. On my way."

While I waited, I went over Henry's study and the pool area once again. Nothing in the study; but in the change shack, which had been clean just the night before, I found a packsack with dirty clothes. Pushed into the back of a closet where the hospitable Borgs kept spare bathing suits, lounging robes, and towels for visitors. No guitar, but there was no question the gear was Martin's. The packsack was moldy, the clothes smelled. No wonder. It had been three months since Martin's death. I squatted in the damp closet, looking at all that remained of the possessions of what by all accounts was a remarkable young man. I remembered Sue's description of him. And the look on Nate's face when he spoke of Martin being special. Fine, special — and dead! No, I wasn't going to let it go, report to James, Katherine, pack up, and go home. No, damn it, I wanted to know! How did he die? Who watched him die — anyone? Shit was going to hit the fan before I left, I promised myself.

By the time Don got to the pool, I was ready for him. I had been tired before but that miserable packsack had given me new energy. It was early evening and cool. I shivered slightly as I made my way slowly back towards the house, carefully observing the pool as I went. It was a standard rectangular 36' by 18', with a diving ramp at the deep end away from the house. A number of wooden outdoor lounge chairs were scattered in no particular order on the surrounding patio.

A long lifesaving pole with a loop on one end hung on the

outside wall of the change shack. I was examining it when Don appeared, all out of breath.

"Hi! What gives? Where's Henry?" he gasped. He was sure out of shape.

"Upstairs. Never mind Henry. Let's you and me have a nice quiet talk, Don. I'm tired of getting the runaround from you folks. Especially you."

"What do you mean, runaround? Look, I may be a bit of a shit in some ways but ...."

"Cut. Please. Save me from that 'forgive me anything because I am cute and harmless' number you play so well. It fools a lot of people but it's run out now. Not only have you been holding out on me, but you've been scheming and plotting all along. Well, it's showdown time."

"Showdown? What's to show? I admitted last night I had been a fool, what more do you want?"

"Still being cute. Okay, here's what I want: what was Gale going to talk to Oscar about when you sent her to his place? What did you see when you followed Martin to his rendezvous with Henry that July evening? And don't tell me you didn't! Sure you did! I should have twigged to that immediately. You knew about Martin and Oscar. No way could you have resisted finding out why Martin was going to talk to Henry. And Martin's gear. What did you do with that? Answers. I want answers. Good answers. Party time's over, Don."

He was taken aback, but then suddenly got aggressive:

"Oh, no you don't! You can't browbeat me. You have no standing here! Who the hell are you to push me around? Katherine will hear of this!"

"So you really are a fool. It's precisely because of Katherine that you'll talk. How will she take being told about Gale? She may not mind you taking a student for a lover but the way you use that girl! And what if I tell her you saw Martin that day and kept mum? Oh no. You have the most to fear and the most to lose if Katherine learns about all this. It's no skin off my nose."

"I can handle Kath, don't you worry. Have for years. She eats out of my hand. Don't you come around with your butch charm trying to make trouble for me with Kath. She isn't susceptible to dykes. Just bugger off and leave us alone!"

"Well, well. Good. Now we're into namecalling. Do you think I haven't heard all that before? Can you really imagine I could be bothered by what you think are insults? Hell, even Henry knows better than that. He's come clean. Now it's your turn."

"Come clean? You mean he confessed?" In spite of his vehemence he sounded surprised.

"No. Henry did not kill Martin."

Donald McPherson stopped in mid-stride and looked around in a panic. He thought he had had it all figured out, but it was coming unstuck.

"But he must have. Or else that jock son of his. I saw him, I saw him!"

"You saw who? Doing what?"

"Oscar, Oscar was here that evening. And then I saw Henry putting a large bundle in the car. They must have done it! They must have!"

"Did you see them together — Oscar and Henry I mean?"

"No." He was thinking, going over his memory slowly. "I wasn't around for all of it. Had to go back for dinner with Kath. But I figured something strange was up so after we ate I walked over through the bush to this house. That's when I saw Oscar. He was running away from here, just crashing through the trees. Towards the county road. He didn't see me. That's what Gale was going to see him about. Just to tell him he had been seen and to suggest he and I talk it over."

"And Henry?"

"Well, I sat down for a while to think it over ...."

"And have a drink. Right?"

"Yeah, I had a mickey stashed in the house. I took it with me. So I took a few pulls at it, had a quiet smoke. Then I went on. There was nobody by the pool, but that pole was off the wall, lying on the ground. So ...."

He stopped and looked at me.

"So you figured someone had needed saving. Or *had not* been saved."

"Something like that. Anyway, I waited around in that hedge. Then I heard someone in the garage; there is direct access between the house and the garage, you know."

"Yeah, I know. Then what?"

"Well, I crept around and I saw Henry stuffing something big into the trunk. The garage door was open, you see, the big door. I saw this bundle, like a body. It could have been a body."

"It was. That was Martin, all right. What else?"

"So how can you say he didn't kill Martin? He must have!"

"Henry just disposed of the body."

"Then Oscar! Oscar for sure. It all fits, right? We have him. Boy, do we have that snotty bastard."

"If you mean Henry, yes, we have him. But not for murder."

"It doesn't matter. Henry or Oscar. It's all one. Listen, what do you intend to do? We can bleed that horse's ass for all he's got. And he's got plenty. Did you know his old man left him $350,000?! Those insurance lawyers really rake it in. So Henry's loaded. We'll be rich!"

"Blackmail's not my kind of caper. And I wouldn't take you for a partner to save my life. Forget it. What did you do with Martin's gear?"

"His gear? I never saw it, except on his back on the road. What about it?"

"Never mind. Perhaps the Sharpes will know about it."

"Yeah. Could be. They were around."

"I thought they were out for the evening that Saturday."

"No, no. I heard them. They left later ...."

"Oh? Okay. I'll ask them. Now tell me again what you did that evening."

Don was all played out. Without further protestation he repeated his story. By the time he left 20 minutes later, I had figured out what had really happened on that hot summer evening of Martin's death.

21

BEFORE I LEFT FOR TORONTO THAT NIGHT I had a confrontation with the Sharpes. Jerry walked up to the house, let himself in, and asked for Henry.

"He's asleep. He's had a hard day. You can talk to him tomorrow."

"Well, you're making yourself right at home, aren't you? Who are you anyway?" He sounded nervous. It was as good a time as any to get him straightened out. So I told him. He was not surprised, but his voice rose a bit and his eyes were uneasy.

"A detective. Does Mr. Borg know you've been making free of the house? You searched it, didn't you?"

"Yes, and guess what I found. But you know don't you? You put it there. Where's the guitar?"

"What guitar? I don't know nothing."

"Martin's gear. Today it's in the change shack, yesterday it wasn't there. Borg didn't put it there. So that leaves you. Why not tell me about it? Get it off your chest. You don't want to be involved in murder, do you?"

"Murder! No, no, we had nothing to do with it, …. if there was a murder. What are you and old man Borg trying to do, blame us? You're in his pay, aren't you? Oh, he would just love to blame everything on the hired help, wouldn't he? How much did he pay you to set us up?"

"Easy. No one is setting you up. Just tell me about the gear and anything else you know and I'll keep you out of it."

By now we were out in front, standing by my truck. Jerry was nervous, kept wiping his hands down his pants. Just then the mobile phone buzzed.

"What's that?" he asked.

"My phone. Take it easy. I won't be a moment."

I opened the door of the pickup and closed it behind me. Jerry lit a ciarette and started to pace up and down on the gravel drive. The sound of his boots on the stones continued through-out my conversation with Alex.

"Hey, your long shots are really coming in," she said. "Here's one: both Martin and Oscar applied for passports. So it looks like they were out to shaft Henry."

"Good for them. What else?"

"This one I can't read. Maybe you can. After I talked to you this afternoon I got hold of Ronnie. Remember Ronnie? At The Fly Trap. Asked him to go to Church Street right away and check for the guitar at the pawnshops there. Second place he went into — Willians' — and there it was! He swears it was Martin's. Knows guitars and knew that one."

"Wow. We did get some luck ...."

"Wait, wait. That's not all. The man in the store remembers who brought it in. A woman. Apparently not very many women pawn guitars. At least not of that quality."

"Could he describe her?"

"Not really, but he said he thought she was young and had an English accent. Didn't you say Molly Sharpe was English?"

"Really. Yes. Makes sense. When was this?"

"Oh, months ago. In July."

"Right. Thanks. I think I can dispose of that now. Listen, Alex, I'll be back soon. Try to see if you can line up Oscar for me. He should have surfaced by now. Get him to your place and sit on him until I get there."

"What if he doesn't want to come? Or stay?"

"You'll think of something. Just do it. Okay?"

"Okay." And she rang off.

I climbed out of the truck and looked at Jerry with some satisfaction. That call from Alex could not have come at a better time.

"There you are. Where were we? Oh, yes. How much did Molly get for tht guitar at Williams? Not very much, I bet."

"Oh my god. I knew it. I knew it. I told her it was too risky. But we needed the money ...."

"Never mind all that. Tell me about where you got it and

when."

"We found it. In the bush. Sort of tucked under a tree out of the way. Over by the road. It must have been there a couple of days. Pack was wet. But the guitar was in a case so it was okay."

"So you hid the pack and sold the guitar. Never told anybody what you found. Didn't you guess they belonged to Martin? And that there would be questions?"

"Not then. Well, we wondered. He had been here that Saturday."

"You eavesdropped, right?"

"I was working in the yard. So I heard the old man offer Martin money. Something like that. It wasn't clear. They were inside. And I couldn't stay; we were meeting some friends for a beer. So I had to leave. I told Molly what I had heard and she made us come home early, just to see that everything was all right, you know."

"Oh, sure."

"Don't believe me if you don't want to, but that's what happened. So we got home early. Borg was around, farting about with the Olds and Martin was gone. So we figured we were too late for the fireworks and just went to bed."

"What time was that?"

"Oh, about 10:00, I guess."

"Okay. And what about the gear?"

"Well, a couple of days later we were out for a walk in the bush. Molly's a great one for walking, being English, and we spotted this pack and guitar. Like I told you. We figured a hiker left it."

"And it never occurred to you it might be Martin's. And might be missed?"

"No! I swear." He was lying through his teeth, which was hardly surprising.

"Never mind. So the temptation was too much, you needed the money. Why didn't you get rid of the pack? It was worthless, right?"

"Right. No, we left it there."

"You left it. Until today?"

"Until today. See we had no idea who you were when you came here before, but then things started happening. Don McPherson was here on Sunday carrying on something fierce with old man Borg ...."

"You just happened to be working in the yard and just happened to overhear ...."

"Yes. Want to make something of it?"

"Not at all. Go on," I laughed. Mollified, he continued.

"Something about Martin disappearing and a woman detective. And other things ...."

"I'll bet."

"And then this morning Molly said you went into the house. Old Borg was here and up early. Obviously waiting for you. And then the two of you left."

"I understand all that. So you put two and two together. But why bring in Martin's gear?"

"It was Molly's idea. She thought it might be a clue. She reads mysteries. Myself, I'm not much of a reader; I prefer TV, but she's big on detective stories and things like that. She thought we should let it be found. We didn't reckon on your having searched the shack before. It seemed a good place to put it. No one has used it much in the last couple of months. So the pack could have been there a long time and then been found accidentally, like."

"Oh, man." I was almost speechless. It's hard to believe anyone could be so dumb.

"So you see, we didn't do nothing."

"Stealing the guitar is nothing?"

"We didn't steal it. Just found it. Molly said, 'finders-keepers'. We didn't know who it belonged to."

He was very unsure of his ground and kept looking around for Molly to show up and support him. Thank god she didn't. One idiot was enough.

Eventually I got a very cowed Jerry back to his house to get

me the pawn ticket, which the two idiots had kept. He came
trotting back with it. I took it, got into the pickup, and split
for Toronto.

22

It took me that night and part of the next day, Tuesday, October 6, to put it all together. Oscar, kept under wraps by Nate and Ronnie by arrangement with the resourceful Alex, supplied some of the missing pieces. Once I had the whole picture the rounding up began.

Nate was toughest. He had retrieved Martin's guitar from the pawnshop and lent me a hand with Don and Oscar, but there his contribution was going to stop. Once he had heard the tale of my trip to Borg's cottage he wanted me to drop the investigation. Or at least to have himself left out of it.

"So now you know where Martin's body is stashed," he said. "What more do you need? You've found him. What does it matter who actually killed him, if it wasn't Borg?"

"It matters to me. And I think it may matter to his parents. It matters so that decisions can be made. Like retrieving Martin's body. A man is dead. What do we tell the authorities? Have to give them somebody."

"Give them Borg. That's what you were going to do, remember? That's what you told me at that dinner we had."

"I was going to give them Borg dead, remember? But he's alive. No, Nate. Sorry. The case is still open until I close it. And right now you're still part of it."

Finally he agreed to co-operate, as a personal favor to me, he said. Actually, his curiosity got the better of his good judgment.

James Millwell was not keen either when I asked him to make himself available. I ran up a hefty phone bill coaxing him.

"Professor, there is no other way. I'm going to get everyone involved together and get at what really happened. I want you there. And bring Sue if you can arrange it. Everyone who cared for Martin should be here for it."

"The denouement. I see." He needed a label.

"The whatever-you-want-to-call-it, yes. It won't be easy in any sense. So please persuade Sue Packer to skip class or whatever and if necessary, pay her way here. The whole thing will be tricky. I'll need your total co-operation."

"But what do you need me or Miss Packer for? We don't know what happened; how can we help?"

"You'll understand that better when it's all over. If it works, that's it. If it doesn't .... well, your trip will be wasted. But surely it's worth it!"

"Of course, of course. How's Katherine taking it all?"

"I think her feelings are still ambiguous. She's not sure whether finding out the truth is worth the pain involved. But I hope she'll realize the necessity. That's why it's important that you and Sue be here. You all cared for Martin."

"Well, you're not being very clear, but persuasive all the same. I'll talk to Miss Packer and offer to fly her down to Toronto. I'll call you back as soon as I have made the necessary arrangements. I take it you want us there as soon as possible. It couldn't wait until the long Thanksgiving weekend, could it?"

"It could not. I would like you here tomorrow, Thursday at the lastest."

"All right. I'll see what I can do," he said, and rang off. James might have appeared cool, but I doubted that he was.

Next, I got in touch with Katherine at her unlisted studio number. I told her that the showdown was imminent and that Millwell was on his way. She was subdued and unco-operative, if not actively hostile.

"All right, all right. I guess you have to move in mysterious ways your wonders to perform. But I don't like it, any part of it. Why all this drama? Either you know what happened or you don't. Isn't this another of your manipulative numbers?"

"Sure it is, what else can it be? Knowing is not enough; it's just a means to an end. Trust me; you have this far. Don't chicken out now, for heaven's sake. Be there."

"I said I would be there so I will. But ...."

I interrupted. "As long as you are, I'll let you know when.

And it will be at the Borg's farm, right next door so it shouldn't be too inconvenient for you."

"Oh, cut it out. 'Inconvenient' indeed." And she hung up on me.

Tuesday was McPherson's day at the FArt, so he was in town. I got a couple of Nate's brawny dudes to keep an eye on him. He was not to disappear or go back to the farm. Chances were good that he would get drunk and stay over until the next day. Then we could pick him up and take him with us. I debated whether to get Gale Mangoni in on the act I was arranging, but decided against it. No point putting her through it.

Meanwhile, Henry was back from Caledon reasonably recovered and trying frantically to get hold of Oscar. Of course he had no luck: Oscar was at Nate's playing checkers with Ronnie.

One way or another, Tuesday was a busy day, and tense. Alex was not much help: she was unhappy and nervous.

"But how do you know it will work? How can you predict what will happen? It's terribly risky," she kept saying.

"I don't and I can't. And of course it's risky. So what? But I could use a little confidence from you. It sure doesn't help to have you so negative."

"I'm sorry, Helen. I guess I'm just not used to this kind of production. The tension is getting me down. Sorry."

"Never mind. We'll pull it off. Waiting and anticipation are always the worst parts. Let's not hassle it anymore."

So to avoid opportunities for hassle I persuaded Alex to go out to see a movie and have a good dinner with a few of her friends. I told her she could afford the money, while I couldn't afford to have her around worrying. She called me names but went. I stayed at her house and waited for word from Millwell. Call finally came. He and Sue Packer would arrive next day.

We were all ready for a showdown at the Borg poolside.

23

NEXT DAY THE WEATHER TURNED BAD and it rained. I dropped Alex off at Henry Borg's to keep him company on the drive to Caledon while I went to pick up Millwell and Packer at the airport. Oscar Borg was to drive up with Nate and Ronnie. McPherson's watchdogs were to bring him along directly to Borg's farm.

Thus it was a convoy of four vehicles that finally parked bumper to bumper in Borg's gravelled driveway. Katherine arrived on foot, gloomy and wet in a yellow slicker. She and Millwell nodded briefly to each other as the rest of us divested ourselves of our raincoats and crowded silently into Henry's study. Don tried to get her attention, to complain about being kidnapped in tones of self-pity, but his attempt was unsuccessful. She ignored him, all her concentration on Sue Packer first and then on Nate Ottoline, the two friends of Martin whom she had never met. Each greeted her quietly, shook hands as if extending condolences at a graveside. Which I guess it was.

The weather had somewhat spoiled my plan to recreate not just the events, but the atmosphere of that Saturday in July. Instead of the sun flooding throught the French doors we saw rain-splattered panes and early fall drabness of fading grass and wilted leaves. It was hard to imagine the hot summer day, the open door, the inviting pool, and the slim, happy young man.

While I took stock, those present arranged themselves with barely a word around the room. Henry presided behind the bar, where he obviously felt more secure and except for an occasional worried glance at Oscar, betrayed little nervousness. Oscar sat huddled next to Ronnie and bit his nails. He looked very handsome and collegiate in his U. of T. leather jacket with "Engineering" on the back and "1980" on the right sleeve. Nate did not sit down. He stood smoking a cigar a little behind the two younger men. That his apparent *sang froid* masked a good deal of tension was betrayed by his busy eyes and the way the cigar rolled around between his fingers. Don, discouraged by Katherine's inattention, had collapsed muttering into a chair behind Henry's desk. His two guardians were sent off to the kitchen by Nate and could be heard there banging pans. James, well trained in tense group situations, acted as if at a faculty meeting, offering drinks and serving them. He finally came to rest with his back to the fireplace, elbow on the mantle. This arrangement left four of us women in the middle of the room surrounded by the silent males. Katherine and Sue refused drinks and sat down next to each other on the couch near James; after a moment of indecision Alex took her drink and found a chair near the door. I remained standing.

"Ladies and gentlemen," I began. A nervous titter ran around the room at this unaccustomed formality. People shifted weight, cleared their throats. The tension relaxed somewhat. I smiled encouragingly and started again. "Okay, then people. We all know why we're here: to find out what happened to Martin Millwell last July. That's the last time he was seen alive. In order to do that we have to go over the situation as it existed last summer. This may seem redundant but it is necessary so we all understand."

"Martin arrived in Toronto, went to Mariposa with Oscar and another young man, Andrew Walec, who is not relevant to this story. There he met Nate Ottoline. That's him with the cigar." Nate's eyes flickered, his head dropped just a fraction in acknowledgment. Everyone looked at him. I went on:

"Martin and Oscar had known each other for four years. Until this summer they had never admitted their mutual attraction. But they had known, even if they had done nothing about it. That right, Oscar?" I asked suddenly. Startled, Oscar squirmed and said, "Yes."

"Yes," I continued, "you both knew it was just a matter of time before you would acknowledge your love and your sexuality. It couldn't be kept under wraps any longer. Martin and

Oscar loved each other. For a couple of weeks this July they were together. Happy, I think."

"What about Ottoline? What was his part in this?" Henry interrupted, hostile. "He put them up to it."

Nate was about to reply but I waved him down.

"You can believe that if it makes you feel better, but rationally, it's unlikely that two grown young men could be turned on to each other against their will. And in the space of a day or two yet, while surrounded by all manner of hetersoxual possibilities. I don't see Nate Ottoline as a villain, even in your terms, Henry. On the contrary, I suspect he let them stay at his place so that the affair could be kept quiet. In case they changed their minds, it was still possible for them to separate with no one the wiser. It was you, Henry, who precipitated the whole tragedy. Your utter insensitivity, your refusal to accept their love as valid. So they planned what many young people had done before them in similar circumstances: they planned to take off, split, go away together. And be damned to you Henry, and your straight anti-life morality." I paused. No one moved, I continued:

"They had no money, but that would not have stopped them. They applied for passports. Ronnie, you have them? Let's see them."

Ronnie took two passports out of his pocket and passed them on to me. I opened both.

"July 22, 1976, two days before Martin's disappearance. They must have applied a couple of weeks before that. Together. That right, Oscar?" Again the lifted head, and the monosyllabic "Yes."

"And right about then Henry Borg did his heavy father number. Oscar knew his father well. He knew that Henry believed that money solved everything and that there was a good chance that he would attempt to bribe Martin. So the two lovers decided to take the bribe and split. That right, Oscar?"

But before Oscar could answer Henry almost screamed at him, Oscar! No! No! Please no! Oscar!"

"Yes, Dad. There didn't seem to be any other way. I knew you would never accept that I'm gay ...."

"You aren't! You couldn't be!"

"But I *am*. And I hate pretending! I hate it, I hate it! Talking about 'chicks' and 'cunts', behaving like you wanted me to — your idea of a man! I hate it! And I won't do it. You can't make me, not any more." Oscar was shaking, his face white with strain and fear. Henry stared at him unbelievingly.

"Oh, my god," he said finally, and fell silent, his eyes still on his son.

I picked up the tale.

"So, when Henry arranged to see Martin at the farm, right in this room in fact, the two conspirators arranged to meet down the road afterwards and take off immediately in Oscar's car. That is why Martin had his gear with him and why he was so cheerful and pleased when Henry offered him $5,000. It was probably much more than they had expected."

"But he didn't have his gear," Henry burst out. "I told you Don lied!"

"No, he didn't. Not about that. Martin left his gear in the bush before he got to your gate. It was found. But that's another story."

"Please, let's get on with it," Katherine said. She had said nothing so far.

"We are; I am," I answered. "It's better to cover the ground as we go. Leave as little out as possible. You see, everyone lied in connection wtih this case. Everyone. Even Sue. Right, Sue? You knew about Oscar and Martin planning to disappear. That's why you weren't too concerned when I came around asking questions."

"Martin wrote me about what had happened between him and Oscar," Sue said. Her voice was low, controlled. "He told me not to be too surprised if he just dropped out of sight. So I wasn't. Except by the time you arrived on the scene, I was starting to wonder why I hadn't heard from him again, wherever he was. He would have written. Then when Professor Millwell told me Oscar was still in Toronto .... well, I knew something was wrong."

At this revelation James made an impatient move.

"You should have told me, Miss Packer. Martin's mother and I had a right to know."

"It was not up to me to tell you. That was Martin's decision." Here, Sue turned to her neighbor. "Anyway, I think Katherine also knew. Didn't you?"

Katherine spoke, not looking at James.

"Yes and no. I knew about Martin and Oscar. I told you that, Helen. I suspected .... but when Martin disappeared and Oscar remained .... I'm sorry, James."

"Yes, you were puzzled," I broke in. "But you didn't want to blow the gaff so you kept quiet. You needn't be apologetic. James Millwell also lied — about Oscar. He also was not sure just what to do. You both tried to keep faith with Martin. It's to your credit."

"That's all very well. Yes, I guessed Oscar had something to do with my son's disappearance. Not because Martin told me, but because I'm not as stupid or insensitive as all parents are alleged to be. I guessed there was latent homosexuality in Martin and I knew he cared for Oscar. Perhaps before *he* did. But I did not know what happened here in Toronto. I had no idea they planned to disappear. I should have been told."

"You have been told. Now. Martin didn't choose to tell you in advance but probably would have called or written once he and Oscar were out of the country. What about that, Oscar?"

"Professor Millwell, I'm sorry. But Martin did intend to let you know. Really. He did love you. But he was afraid you would try to stop us ...."

I decided that was enough of that, or we would be there in that depressing study all day. So I interrupted.

"That's all what-might-have-been. What we need to get to the bottom of this is what actually happened. So let's go back to that Saturday. Martin met Don on the road. Don was curious, decided to eavesdrop on the meeting ...."

McPherson suddenly came alive. "No, no. That's not what I told you I didn't get here until later. Much later. When I saw Oscar running away. Ask him what he was doing here ...."

"We know what he was doing. He was waiting for Martin. Okay, Oscar, tell us what happened that day as far as you know."

"It was awful. Awful. I saw Martin .... dead .... in the pool." I interrupted.

"No. Start before that. Where were you to meet? Why did you come up to the house? Wasn't that risky? Your father might have seen you."

Here Henry started to say something, but I stopped him.

"You'll have your say, Henry. Hold it. Let's hear Oscar now."

"All right," said Oscar. "I came down in the wagon and left it at the garage in Orangeville. I had my Mustang there, being serviced. So I picked it up and drove to the county road one concession over. I was supposed to wait for Martin there. But I got anxious and curious and excited, so I walked across the fields at the back of the house here. I didn't want anyone to see me so I kept to the bush. And when I got here Martin was dead! I just got scared and ran ...."

"And that's when Don McPherson saw you?"

"Guess so."

"What else did you see at the pool?"

"Martin, just Martin. In the water. That's all I saw."

"How did you know he was dead? How could you?"

Before Oscar could reply Don broke in.

"He's lying! There was no body in the pool. After I saw him I went straight there and the pool was empty. There was just the pole, which made me curious. Oscar must have taken Martin out with it, that's how he knew Martin was dead. He killed him!"

"But why, Don? Why would Oscar kill Martin? He had no motive. We'll come back to you. Now, Henry, let's have your version. Tell us all you did that evening."

"I aleady told you."

"Tell me again, Henry. Tell us all."

"I gave Martin the money, he went out to the pool, and I stayed inside. In the kitchen and upstairs. Must have been 10 to 15 minutes. Then when I came out Martin was in the water. So I went in and got him out. He was dead."

"Were there any marks on him? Bruises, blood?"

"I didn't see any. I thought it was an accident. The pole was on the ground, but I didn't think to use it. Anyway, I pulled him out, got a blanket, put everything back the way it was and then I carried him and his clothes to the garage, to the trunk of my car. Next day I drove up to the cottage and when my wife and Oscar left the day after, I .... but you know all that!"

"We'll get back to what you did with the body later. Now, we need to know why. Why did you dispose of the body? If you didn't kill Martin, why?"

"I told you that before. Oscar. I was afraid he would show up and not believe me. I admit it was dumb but understandable. I'm sorry now, but that's all I could think of at the time."

"You had it all planned, didn't you? Well in advance. Let's take your story of Oscar's call from the cottage. That's a lie, Henry. There's no record of that call. So how could you have thought Oscar would suddenly arrive?"

"He did call ...."

"Yes, but not until after you had hidden Martin's body. He called on his way back to the cottage. He was upset, wanted to know what had happened. And you told him Martin had left. He knew that was not true. But that was the only time he called that day. No Henry, your story of a sudden brainstorm leading you to dispose of Martin's body just won't wash. It's not your style. You had planned to kill Martin if he didn't accept your bribe. You were all ready to do the deed when he surprised you by accepting. That's why you had to go away by yourself and cool down. You had worked yourself up to do murder and now you had to cancel. It's hard on the nerve endings."

McPherson couldn't contain himself. He yelled:

"He did it, of course he did it! Motive or no, he was all hetup for it so he did it!"

Henry answered him before I could.

"No. I did not kill Martin. I came down and there he was dead in the pool. I couldn't believe it for a moment — as if it had happened just because I had planned it! Helen's right, I would have done it, but I didn't"

"Go on, then," I said, looking at Katherine rather than at Henry. It was her son we were talking about.

"I had had it all planned. As a contingency. I worked out exactly what I would do it .... So when I found him dead I just put the rest of the plan into action."

"Weren't you interested or concerned about who had killed him? It did change things, surely. You were not in full control. There was another factor to consider."

"I guess I believed at the time it was an accident. And .... and I already felt guilty. Don't you see? I could never have pulled off an accident story because I had murder on my own mind. I could not have acted innocent because in my heart I wasn't. Don't you see?"

"I see," said Katherine. "I see, and it just blows my mind. That you could calmly plan to kill a human being! Because he was gay and loved your son! Is that a reason to kill? It's too much ...." She fell silent again.

Henry said nothing. Tension in the room intensified. It was Nate Ottoline who broke the silence.

"How do we know it wasn't in fact an accident? I know Martin was a good swimmer, but accidents do happen. A sudden muscle spasm, momentary blackout. It was hot, Martin had just had a drink. What makes you believe he was killed?" This was addressed to me.

"Because of inconsistencies — especially in timing. I told you everyone has lied. Some stories just do not jibe. And the pole tells us it was no accident. The lifesaving pole. What was it doing off its hook?"

"What doesn't jibe?" asked James.

Before I could answer, Don broke in again.

"If it wasn't Henry then it must have been Oscar! I told you! He was there!"

"No. He was not the only one who was there Don."

Don got the message. The pole, the timing, the other person who was there: himself.

He jumped up, dashed to the French doors, and tried to open them. Until he saw through the rain the figures of his two ex-companions. They were no longer in the kitchen, banging pans. They were outside on the patio. Making sure there was no escape.

24

It took a while to get the situation under control. Donald McPherson had collapsed in hysteria. Now all his words were for Katherine. She sat dry-eyed, watching and listening to his pathetic explanation. There really wasn't much to his story. He had gotten to the house just as the Sharpes were driving away. He had told me that. And that was just when Martin had entered the pool. He knew or guessed something of the situation between Martin, Oscar, and Henry. He was overwhelmingly pleased at the pain it was causing Henry and was trying to think of a way to turn it to his advantage. Seing Martin happy and alone in the pool, he grabbed the pole and with the loop over Martin's head, forced him underwater. It was that simple; an impulsive act brought on by hatred of Henry, resentment of Martin, years of booze and self-pity.

"Why, Don, why did you kill my son?" Katherine finally managed to ask.

"He was young and happy and you cared more for him than for me," Don sobbed out and went on hating and justifying and justifying and hating. Tough, hardnosed Nate just couldn't bear it any longer. He forced a full glass of neat whiskey down Don's throat and had his two henchmen carry him out of the room.

"That's enough," Nate said, "Miss Payne doesn't have to take any more of that. Take him away. Now Helen, now that you have made us go through all this, what's next?"

Everyone turned to me, almost accusingly. I had indeed made them go through a lot and could not expect anyone to be grateful. On the contrary, it seemed I was to blame for it, and certainly was expected to clean it up. It isn't just guns that make mine a tough way to make a living.

It was Sue who somewhat defused the situation.

"What I want to know is how you knew. What gave him away?

It's easy to see it all now, but how did you arrive at it?"

I smiled at her gratefully.

"It's really not so easy to make up a consistent lie. First of all there is the pole. Being off the hook suggests it was not an accident, right? Then Don made up this silly story about getting to the pool after Martin's body had been removed and seeing the pole on the ground. But Henry had tucked it away by then. Don wanted to tie Oscar to the time and place but didn't want to admit that he himself had actually seen Martin dead. He never saw the pool with Martin gone. He was only at the pool that one time, when he killed Martin. I knew that because he let it slip that he heard the Sharpes leaving. Martin was alone then. And it never occurred to Don that Henry would put the pole away."

"But he did see Oscar running through the bush?"

"Oh, yes. Probably as he was on his way back to his house. After the murder. Not near the pool at all. If Oscar had arrived at the pool a few minutes earlier, well .... things might have been different. Like Don says, 'luck of the drunk'."

"Luck! My, you have a macabre sense of humor."

I let that comment go. It was time to face the consequences of what we all now knew.

"You must see now why all this was necessary. Katherine, I'm sorry to have put you through all this. But you did protect him, and would have gone on protecting him. It was essential that you realize just who and what he is. You'll have to readjust your life; it'll be hard. And this mess is not over yet. That's why Sue and James are here. It affects them too. There are decisions you must make. Go to the cops? If so, what do we tell them? If not, what do we do about Don? And how do you feel about Henry's part in this? What about Martin's body? Except for Borg, you all cared for Martin in one way or another. It's up to you to decide together. I'll abide by your decision."

I moved towards the door. Alex was already half out of the room. There was no way I was going to let them off that hook. I was tired. After all, it was their mess. But it wasn't to be so easy. Their collective hostility dropped in the face of my impending departure. They wanted my 'advice' they said; I must stay and help them decide. Even Alex changed her line and got into the act.

"Look, you can't just leave them like this. They're babes in the woods. And right now some of them are badly traumatized."

"So what do you want me to do? Make decisions for them? Those who'll have to live with the consequences are the only ones qualified to make decisions. It won't make much difference to me either way. The cops may not like what I've done, but they can't touch me. For Borg and the rest, it's different."

James Millwell now spoke up.

"What about if we don't get the police in on it, what then?"

"You'll have to do something about Don. That at least. Don't you want to bring up your son's body? How about how Oscar feels about that? Can Martin just disappear?"

"Although I'm not directly involved," Sue spoke up, "at least as far as the cops are concerned, my advice is to keep the cops and publicity out of it. If you don't all your lives will be hell for years. Don't trust the cops."

"Yes, yes. That's all very well. We see the problems in that. But then what do we do?"

"Okay. Since you want me to help you, I will." I suddenly decided to get it over with. "You have a clear choice: either get Martin's death out of your hands, go to the cops and take the consequences, get good lawyers and sit tight. Or .... take on the full burden of dealing with what's happened. For that the minimum is that you trust each other, and each contribute to whatever needs to be done. Could you do that? Because if you decide that you can, then I'm sure we can come up with a plan for how to do it. It's not the logistics that are the problem, it's you. Do you have the trust and the guts?"

As the implication of what I was saying sank in, they looked around at each other. Henry Borg, who had the most to lose if the police were called in, was the first to come up with a concrete idea and an offer to implement it.

"If you would let me. Yes, I'm sure I could arrange for Martin's body to show up in the lake and be called an accident. I know the locals, the cops, the coroner. It's known that we've been looking for him for months. He could have had an accident in July while alone at my cottage, swiming. How about that?"

"You sure you could swing it?"

"Yes, yes. If you would let me. Would that be all right, Katherine? Then he could be properly buried .... I guarantee it. Leave it to me."

"That seems appropriate," Sue said. She was holding Katherine's hands in hers.

"Okay. It would need working out, but it sounds promising. Any ideas .... about Don?"

Here Nate stepped in.

"I don't know how Miss Payne feels about him .... but ...."

Katherine broke in.

"Right now I don't feel. At all. I can't understand how we could have lived together so long with me not knowing how he felt. I guess I feel responsible ...."

"Nuts." Alex was not about to let this go. "Feel sorry for him, okay. But responsible! Never. He's obviously badly disturbed. And an alcoholic. Dangerous. What were you going to suggest, Nate?"

"Yes, Mr. Ottoline, what? I don't know what would be best myself so I'll certainly go along with any reasonable idea."

"It's not my place exactly, but since as Alex says he's disturbed, it would not be too hard to dispose of him ...."

"Kill him, you mean? Another murder? No!"

"Not necessarily. I had in mind more like a private institution. There are such places. Many families have members whom they wish to keep out of the way. I could look into it. There are such things as 'tame' doctors. It could be arranged."

"Convict him and lock him up for the duration, is that it?" asked James.

"Until he dies of drink. Yes. It needn't be any snakepit, you know. Quite pleasant, really."

"May I make a suggestion?" said Sue.

"Go ahead."

"Why don't we ask him. It's his life we're talking about. Surely he has some rights!"

"Well said, Sue," said Katherine, suddenly animated.

"Now, what can that mean? It doesn't make sense. Murderer, a maniac, and a drunk ...." Henry couldn't believe his ears.

In the hubbub, no one noticed that Oscar had not said a word. Now he spoke up.

"Ask him, go ahead, ask him. Here in front of us all. I want to see him. I want to see the man who murdered Martin."

Nate nodded to Ronnie, who went out. The room fell silent. In a few minutes Ronnie was back. He seemed uncertain.

"Well?" asked Nate. "Where is he?"

"He seems to be in a coma. Maybe it's just the whiskey we gave him. I couldn't find his heartbeat."

I was out of the room in a flash, Ronnie following. The others remained, still and tense. Don was in an upstairs bedroom sprawled on a bed. I checked him over; his pulse, his eyes. Ronnie stood and watched me in silence. Finally I looked up at him. His eyes were steady, his voice firm when he spoke.

"Heart attack."

"Heart attack." I said. We stared at each other for perhaps another 15 seconds. Then I walked past him down the stairs and into the hushed study.

"Henry." I said, "Get your tame medic. Don is dead."

"Hallelujah," somebody said quietly.

THE END